DANIEL HAYES

Flyers

ALADDIN PAPERBACKS

ALSO BY DANIEL HAYES

THE TROUBLE WITH LEMONS
EYE OF THE BEHOLDER
NO EFFECT

First Aladdin Paperbacks edition May 1998

Copyright © 1996 by Daniel Hayes

Aladdin Paperbacks
An imprint of Simon & Schuster Children's Publishing Division
1230 Avenue of the Americas
New York, NY 10020

Also available in a Simon & Schuster Books for Young Readers
hardcover edition.
Designed by Anahid Hamparian
The text for this book was set in 10-point Leawood Book.
Printed and bound in the United States of America
10 9 8 7 6 5 4 3 2

The Library of Congress has cataloged the hardcover edition
as follows:
Hayes, Daniel.
Flyers / Daniel Hayes. — 1st ed.
p.   cm.
Summary: While filming a movie for a school project, Gabe and his
friends discover mysterious activities at a supposedly vacant house.
ISBN 0-689-80372-9 (hc.)
[1. High schools—Fiction. 2. Schools—Fiction. 3. Friendship—Fiction.
4. Grandfathers—Fiction. 5. Death—Fiction.] I. Title.
PZ7.H31415Fl 1996
[Fic]—dc20   96-10568
ISBN 0-689-80373-7 (pbk.)

Flyers

One

I'll start with the night Rosasharn attacked Ray McPherson's car near the entrance to Blood Red Pond. Not that Rosasharn's dressing up as some kind of creature from the Black Lagoon and hurling himself onto the hood of Ray's old Buick had much to do with what followed, but looking back on it, I realize that was when I got my first small sign that something was going on around there. Something strange. And I don't mean Rosasharn's behavior, which may seem strange to you but was pretty much par for the course for him. I'm talking about the other things, the things that started happening later.

But I'd better backtrack a little here. You're probably wondering why Rosasharn was decked out in a swamp thing costume that night in the first place, and in the second place, what inspired him to ambush Ray and his car the way he did. The costume part is easy enough to explain, but the other—well, you'd kind of have to know Rosasharn to understand that.

The costume was from a film my friend Bo and I were making as our summer G&T project. G&T stands for Gifted and Talented, although I'm not sure I'm either, and if you were to take a peek at my report card, you wouldn't exactly be thinking Rhodes scholar. Supposedly, though, I have all this untapped potential, and G&T people love nothing more than to get their mitts on underachievers. Plus Bo was a definite shoo-in for the G&T program, and I wouldn't be surprised if his mom, who teaches English at the high school, pulled some strings for me. Bo and I had always been a team—not only in our film projects, but in general as well.

Anyway, Rosasharn had the title spot in our film, which we were calling *Green Guy Gets Therapy*. We had plenty of time, since the regular school year wasn't even over yet and we wouldn't be turning our project in till fall, but you never know what kinds of problems or delays you might run into on a film. Our last effort, *Rogue Nun*, still isn't done and I'm not sure it ever will be, at least not as long as Father Ryan is pastor at St. Mary's. He acts nice enough when he sees me, but I can sense a definite difference there since back in March when a few dozen of our extras practically trampled him in the foyer of his own church, and on St. Patrick's Day, no less, as he'd pointed out to Pop that night at Willie's. He hadn't been all that keen on letting us use the church for filming to begin with, and no doubt would have nixed the idea from the start if I'd told him the film's title, *or* that it involved a nun who goes berserk at mass one Sunday morning with a small arsenal she's been building up under her habit since the days when they still said the mass in Latin. I had told him we weren't sure of the title yet, which wasn't an outright lie since we never are sure until we wrap things up, and that it was basically the story of an aging sister who missed the way things used to be. Bo said at the time I should be more up front with the guy, but my thinking had been that the church scenes were just too crucial to risk that kind of reckless honesty. And I still say it would have worked out if Father Ryan had stayed on schedule. Was it my fault he had to come back early from his Saturday hospital rounds in Cambridge and poke his nose in the church just as we were shooting the stampede of parishioners fleeing the wrath of Sister Violet and one of her semiautomatics?

Our *Green Guy* flick was pretty much in the same vein as the nun thing—a campy, semi-horror piece, sort of a *Lost Boys* meets *Young Frankenstein*. After that sticky business with Father Ryan, I was determined to keep things low-key, this time writing a script that was set in the country and didn't require extras, who, even when they don't mow down a priest, ruin a lot of good shots by laughing and waving at the camera and generally making a pain of themselves.

That night should have been a piece of cake. By eight o'clock we'd pretty much finished setting up camp on a little hill overlooking Blood Red Pond. Bo had taken his video camera down to the water's edge hoping to get some good atmosphere shots of the sunset. I had a decent campfire going and my little brother Ethan had finished making sure we had everything we needed for the scenes we'd be shooting. You might say Ethan functioned as our producer. Even at eleven he had the kind of mind for detail that Bo and I could only dream of having. It'd be just like us to show up for a shoot with no batteries, no videotape, and no camera. Ethan made sure that didn't happen.

"I think we're all set, Gabe," Ethan announced after checking things over one more time. He waited to see if I needed him for anything else, then reached down and fished a comic out of his backpack. The next thing I knew he was facedown, propped up on his elbows, and lost in another Superman adventure.

Not long after that, I heard what could only have been Rosasharn's arthritic old Ford dragging itself up the lane toward us. It was probably all in my imagination, but whenever that car pulled up I had the feeling that in addition to all the creaking and rattling and backfiring, I could hear Jeremy and Rosasharn bickering inside. Or I should say Jeremy bickering and Rosasharn coming up with new and original ways of giving him things to bicker about. They were the unlikeliest duo you could ever imagine. Rosasharn was actually Billy Rosa but we'd renamed him in fourth grade after seeing Rosasharn the hillbilly girl in *The Grapes of Wrath*. Our Rosasharn was a good-natured Hoss Cartwright type who couldn't have been any more different from the sad-sack *Grapes of Wrath* Rosasharn if he tried, but the name stuck nonetheless. Jeremy was Jeremy Wulfson, a wiry-looking, impatient-acting sort of guy who usually walked around with such a blazing scowl he'd actually developed well-defined muscles in his face. He and Rosasharn had been a team for as long as Bo and I had.

"Greetings, Gabriel Riley, o great writer of swamp epics and creator of killer nuns," Rosasharn said, climbing out of the car and giving me a deep bow.

"Hi, scrub," Jeremy said, and got out too. Right away he started scrounging around the campsite, looking to see what was in the cooler we'd brought and what kinds of things were lying around on the ground. He halted his inspection when he got to Ethan. "Ya reading Tarzan again?" he asked, scowling down at him.

"Superman," Ethan told him, looking up at him with big, serious eyes as if it were the first time Jeremy'd ever asked that question. One time a few years earlier, Jeremy had made the mistake of thinking it was Tarzan comic books that Ethan was always reading, and he'd gotten a charge out of the way Ethan had solemnly explained how it was Superman he liked, not Tarzan. Then Ethan had gone on to explain that while he didn't have anything against Tarzan personally, if you looked at the facts, you'd see that Tarzan was totally different from Superman and really couldn't even be considered in the same league. "Besides," he'd said, delivering what was to him the clincher, "Tarzan can't *fly*." After that, whenever Jeremy saw Ethan with a comic book, which was pretty often, he'd ask if it was Tarzan.

Jeremy gave a shrug. "Superman, Tarzan—same difference."

Ethan studied him a minute, and then, probably deciding this wasn't the day he'd finally get through to him, went back to Superman.

A few seconds later, as if to illustrate the point Ethan would have liked to have made, Rosasharn sailed past us on an old Tarzan swing Bo and I had put up years before. We heard about three quarters of a Tarzan yell, then a little snap, and the next thing we knew Rosasharn had crash-landed in the dirt. Something like that is funny enough in itself, but Rosasharn topped it off by lying there clutching the broken rope and giving another Tarzan yell as if he were still flying along at a mile a minute. Ethan looked up and smiled, which was good to see because I often worried that Ethan was a little too serious for a kid his age.

"Maybe you should use public transportation, Rosasharn," I said, reaching down to help him up.

"Maybe he should lose weight," Jeremy added.

I suggested that Rosasharn get into his Green Guy outfit and started down the hill to see how Bo was coming along. Behind me I heard Jeremy give a yelp and turned to see Rosasharn with a long stick and a Three Musketeers pose. *"En garde,"* he said, and did a little fancy footwork.

"Go ahead, ya tub," Jeremy told him, picking up a

club-sized piece of wood. "I'll duel ya. I'll duel ya right across the head." He moved in with the chunk of wood until Rosasharn retreated, giving him a Curly-of-the-Three-Stooges wave-off. "I thought so," Jeremy said.

Ethan had looked up from his comic book and was giving another little smile.

"Go back to reading Tarzan," Jeremy told him.

I watched as Bo panned the camera north to south, catching the sunset glinting off the water. Everything down by the pond was so peaceful, as if all of nature were holding its breath. I knew that evening and early morning were Bo's favorite times to be at Blood Red Pond. Mine too, although mornings I'm usually in no mood to appreciate things. Bo and I had practically grown up around that pond. Pop had bought the farmhouse along with the land that bordered the pond before he'd gotten married and moved up from his old stomping grounds in South Troy, which he joked was never quite the same after the last of the Irish breweries went under. And although Mr. Lindstrom, an old widower who owned the land that the pond was on, wasn't exactly crazy about mankind, referring to people in general as "them sons-o'-bitches," he took to Pop right away and loved to take him on walking tours showcasing the improvements he was constantly making on his land, one of which was the pond itself. Pop remembers when it was a simple pond in the woods, but when I was still in diapers Mr. Lindstrom bulldozed the outlet so the water would back up and flood the surrounding area. He wanted it to be a sort of nature preserve for ducks and geese and beavers and whatever. There had been an outcry from some of the townspeople at the time because the pond was considered to have some historical significance, supposedly being the site of a brutal Indian massacre way back in the days of the French and Indian War. There was some argument about whether the massacre had ever actually happened, and even among those who believed it had, there was disagreement about whether the Indians had been the massacre-ers or the massacre-ees. Nonetheless, popular legend had it that the pond had turned red with blood from all who died there on that fateful day, whoever they were.

Other legends about the place had sprung up over the years, supported by a couple of centuries of sporadic eyewitness testimony. These eyewitness reports ranged from descriptions of Indian ghosts to unexplained lights swirling over the water on moonless nights. My favorite story (and probably the one that gave me the idea for our film) was that a bizarre swamp creature, a little like a man but a lot like something else, was headquartered there. Every few generations somebody would claim to have been scared out of a decade or two of his allotted lifespan by having had a late-night encounter with this guy, who everybody agreed was anything but friendly.

These stories emanating from around Blood Red Pond added a kind of mystique to the place that I thoroughly enjoyed—almost as much as I enjoyed its wild beauty. For his part, Mr. Lindstrom didn't give two hoots about the massacre legend, or the supernatural sightings, or, for that matter, the outcry from concerned citizens that by plugging up the outlet he was tampering with a piece of local history, however murky and unsubstantiated. Pop recalls the day he started up his bulldozer, mumbled something about "them sons-o'-bitches," and went to work, making the pond pretty much what it is today.

As you might expect from Mr. Lindstrom's apparent lack of fondness for the human race, the property was off-limits to everyone from bird-watchers to hunters, not to mention the amateur historians. Pop was always welcome though, and Ethan and I were too. Mr. Lindstrom once told Pop that he liked to look at us as his own kids, the only ones he had left, and he hoped Pop didn't mind. Pop told him he was pleased to hear him say it because he wasn't all that confident he could do a good enough job with us on his own. Mr. Lindstrom didn't mind our friends being there either, but I was careful never to take anybody there who hunted or drank or did anything else he might not approve of. I think he appreciated this because a couple of summers ago he gave me my own key to the barn where he kept his old wooden rowboat so we could use that whenever we wanted to. A few weekends earlier, we'd wheeled the boat over to the pond and I rowed while Bo sat in front and filmed as we glided past the dead tree trunks that were still sticking up out of the water—a reminder that most of the swamp used to be woods. The footage we got was outstanding. To see the tape, you'd swear we'd been gliding through some kind of Louisiana bayou that was teeming with alligators and water moccasins and God knows what else. And that was before we'd added sound effects.

Bo finished panning and gave me a little over-the-shoulder wave, which took me by surprise since I hadn't made a sound as far as I could tell. That was more like what I expected from Ethan, who seemed to have a sixth sense about that kind of thing. It was almost impossible to sneak up on Ethan, who was always doing things like answering our door before anybody even rang the bell—just the opposite of Pop and me, who might not know the difference if somebody was out there taking our front porch apart.

Bo must have noticed my surprised expression. "You're not half as quiet as you think you are, Gabe." He reached down and grabbed his camera bag.

"You may want to stay here for a while," I told him. "Rosasharn and Jeremy are going at it again."

Bo laughed. "Or maybe we'd better get started while they're both still in one piece." He slid the camera bag over my shoulder and picked up his camera and tripod.

"You want to check on your dad first?" Bo asked as we started up the hill. "We can hold off on the shooting."

"Nah," I said. "It's early. I'll do it after."

Bo nodded and we trudged on. A few seconds later we heard some yelling and looked up the hill to see Rosasharn rolling on the ground in front of the campfire. I thought at first he was doing that Curly thing where he gets on the ground and runs his feet around in circles, until I saw Jeremy tear over and start swatting at him. Then Ethan jumped up and got into the act. Bo and I ran up to see what the deal was.

"The stupid tub was on fire," Jeremy told us, still a little out of breath.

Little wisps of smoke rose up from the ankles of Rosasharn's Green Guy costume.

"He was moonwalking," Ethan explained, wide-eyed. "And he went through the fire."

"It was the fire's fault," Rosasharn announced from the ground. "It should have seen me coming."

"Stupid tub," Jeremy said, all indignant. "How's a fire s'posed to see you coming?" That was the beauty of Jeremy: No matter how ridiculous a situation got, he always insisted on being rational. That alone probably went a long way toward explaining his scowl.

I bent down to study Rosasharn's smoldering outfit, a sickly olive-green thing that had been designed and manufactured by Rosasharn's girlfriend, Sudie Robinson. The costume consisted of a pair of gray long johns covered with pea-green construction paper scales, along with matching green gloves, and a Halloween headpiece we'd picked up at a costume shop in Schenectady. Some of the scales below the knees were pretty well charred, and we didn't have any paper on hand to fix them up. I reported all this to Bo.

"Hmm . . . ," Bo said, thinking. "Why don't we go out to the road for the car scene. It'll be dark enough by the time we're set up there, and it's almost all long shots and facials so you won't be able to see his ankles much anyway."

He reached down to help Rosasharn to his feet. "You still up for this, tiger?"

"Me health has niver been better," Rosasharn said in a lousy Irish accent. "And me mither thanks ya fur inquirin'."

"Stupid tub," Jeremy said. And in a strange way his grumpiness was kind of touching. I think he'd been genuinely worried for the big guy.

Jeremy sat there for a minute rotating the steering wheel back and forth and scowling at it. "Is this thing attached to anything?" he wanted to know.

Bo and I laughed. The play in Rosasharn's steering wheel was legendary. We used to joke that you had to turn it three complete revolutions to switch lanes. The rest of the car was no great shakes either. The transmission, an archaic on-the-column three-speed, was exactly fifty percent shot, having a second and third gear but no first or reverse. Not only that, but the floor of the car had, over the years, gradually rusted away from the sides, which left it strung there like a hammock, and when you hit bumps it sagged down and gave you a good view of the pavement flying by underneath.

"Okay, start it up," I told Jeremy as Bo went over to help Ethan, who was setting up the video camera. "Pump the gas a few times first."

"Shuddup," Jeremy said. "I know how to drive." He did. Being a farm kid, he'd probably done more driving than all of us put together, but since he was now driving for our film I felt justified in giving him advice.

Jeremy pushed the brake, which you could tell from the way he scrunched down sank almost to the floor. "Ya call this a car?" he said.

The engine turned over slowly as Jeremy hit the key, and with a belch of smoke started up. It sat there wheezing and shaking like something sick that needed to have a blanket thrown over itself.

"Okay," I said, sticking my head in the window. "Remember, no reverse, so you'll just hang a U-ey in my driveway. And be careful on the hill. The road has some major dips there and with this steering, you could lose it. And the most important thing—are you listening, Jeremy?—the most important thing is you gotta be able to stop when Rosasharn jumps in front of you. You already know about the brakes, so give yourself room. Ya hear me?" I reached in and rapped on his head a few times.

He slapped my hand away. "Nobody'd stop for that," he said, pointing at Rosasharn, who was coming toward us in his Green Guy getup.

"Just follow the script, Jeremy. When he jumps in front of you, stop. Humor me on this one."

"Greetings from the swamp world," Rosasharn said.

"Nobody'd stop for that," Jeremy said again, and shoved the car in gear. Then, tromping down on the gas, he feathered the clutch and tried to coax the car forward. From the sound, you'd've thought it was the space shuttle lifting off. A few seconds later the car started moving. You might have had the feeling you were watching the whole scene in slow motion except the car was shaking like crazy and Jeremy seemed to be scowling at his usual speed.

I stepped back out of the smoke cloud and watched the car limp up the hill. When it made the top, I started in on Rosasharn. "Remember," I told him, "stay outta camera range until the car gets close and then come charging into its field of vision. You can stay behind that bush over by the barn until it's time."

"Zay will not drive zee car past my swamp," Rosasharn told me. "Zay must be stopped."

"Yeah, well make sure zay don't run over you," I cautioned him.

Rosasharn shuffled off toward his bush and I headed over to where Bo and Ethan were. The way we had it planned was that on Jeremy's first run Bo would shoot a long shot of the attack from the entrance lane. Ethan had already turned on the yard light that was attached to the peak of the old barn. Bo figured the yard light, along with the headlights on Rosasharn's car, should give the scene a kind of glary, shadowy effect, where you'd see Green Guy, but not too clearly, which was important considering how ratty he looked, especially in the ankle department. Then we'd have Jeremy do a couple more runs for shots from different angles, and finally Bo'd get some footage from inside the car looking out the windshield.

I ran over and stood behind Ethan, trying to picture how it all might come out. I'd written it, but I wasn't too sure how it would translate onto film. As usual I had to trust Bo to make it look right.

Bo knew what I was thinking and laughed. "We'll get what we get," he said. That pretty much summed up Bo's whole approach to life, and it was one of the things I really admired about him. Most people our age fell into two categories: They either didn't care about things at all, or if they did, they were completely neurotic about them. Bo really poured himself into pretty much everything he did; he just didn't worry very much about how things panned out. Even so, I'd bet dollars to doughnuts that no filmmaker in the country his age was doing better work than Bo Michaelson.

Right after I finished thinking this, I noticed a set of headlights shooting up over the hill Jeremy had just disappeared behind.

"That can't be him already," I said. "Can it?"

We stood there watching as a car cleared the hill.

"It's not him," Bo said. "Listen."

He was right. What we were hearing was a regular car, the kind of car Rosasharn's would never sound like again.

It was bearing down on us.

"Let's get outta sight," I said, "so whoever it is doesn't stop and ruin the shot when Jeremy shows up."

Ethan was already picking up the camera bag, and Bo grabbed the camera and tripod. We all hurried toward the barn.

"Sit tight, Rosasharn," I said as we ducked into the barn.

"Zay will not drive zee car past my swamp!" we heard Rosasharn say.

"It's not *Jeremy*, Rosasharn!" I hissed out the door. "Stay put!"

"Zay must be stopped!"

I looked at Bo. He looked back at me and shrugged. Ethan crept up to the only window on the road side of the barn and peeked out. Bo was next. Soon all three of our faces were pressed up against the glass.

At first we couldn't see the actual car, only the light it cast on the trees and bushes alongside the road. We could see Rosasharn, though, crouched behind his bush right off to the side from our window, and two seconds later we heard what might have been a cross between a Tarzan yell and a moose in heat, and our man Rosasharn was on the move. He charged onto the road, planted his feet, and held up his hands like some kind of underworld traffic cop. The car, which I recognized right away as Ray McPherson's—an old wreck of a Buick stitched together with Bondo and a colorful mixture of preowned fenders—screeched to a halt in front of him. Before the front end had quit bobbing, Rosasharn was on the hood and heading for the windshield. He was making some kind of barking noise and clapping his hands together.

"He's doing that seal thing he does," I heard from Bo, whose head was just the other side of Ethan's. For someone who takes things pretty much in stride, he sounded fairly amazed.

It *was* a sight to behold. Rosasharn was sitting up on the hood as if he were waiting for a fish to be dropped in his mouth. At that point Ray must've all of a sudden snapped out of it because he hit reverse and gunned it, sending Rosasharn out of his seal pose and into a backward roll. He landed on the pavement, and the car screeched out of our range of vision and made what sounded like a power U-turn. A few seconds later it was history.

We ran out to check on Rosasharn. He was up on all fours when we got to him.

"Woof," he said, being a dog now and looking to where the car had disappeared over the hill.

"You all right, killer?" Bo asked, patting his head.

"Woof," he said, and gave us a nod.

We helped him to his feet and brushed him off a little.

"I can't believe you, Rosasharn," I said, laughing. "You're *crazy*."

"Yes," he said, tilting his head and pointing his finger philosophically, "but still I must protect zee swamp."

We were still laughing about that when I noticed Ethan staring out into the trees across the road with that look he gets every once in a while. Whatever he thought he saw, *I* couldn't see. But that was when it all began. At least for me it was.

TWO

It was pushing ten o'clock by the time we finished filming out by the road. Jeremy had pulled up about three minutes after Rosasharn had rolled off Ray's hood and was a little put out when Rosasharn wasn't immediately available to jump in front of him. We were busy doing what on-the-spot repairs we could on his battered-up Green Guy outfit and didn't pay much attention when Jeremy actually rolled up.

"Aren't we *forgetting* something?" we heard him ask. You could almost feel him glaring out the window at us.

Bo and I put on puzzled looks.

"I don't think so," I said. "We forgetting something, Bo?"

Bo shrugged. "I can't think of anything."

"Idiots," Jeremy said. Then he made us pay for our fun by refusing to drive the car anymore until I practically had to beg.

That wasn't my only problem. All while we were shooting the car attack scene from different angles I kept expecting Ray to show up again—with some kind of homemade posse, maybe, or maybe alone but carrying a shotgun or some such thing, and then we'd have some serious explaining to do. Ray was that chain-smoking, emaciated type, a nice enough guy for the most part, but temperamental (I'd heard some use the word *crazy*), and emaciated-looking or not, had been known to do serious damage to people when he was in one of his moods. I'd always gotten along well with Ray, but he was one boat I didn't want to rock.

Luckily that was the last we saw of him—that night at least.

When we finally wrapped up, I was surprised at how much time had passed and figured I should see about Pop— whether he'd made it home or not and how he was doing. I wasn't sure exactly what the story was but for the last few weeks it seemed that Pop had needed a little extra looking after. He'd always been what you might call the life of the party, and as far back as I could remember we'd sometimes had to go out in the middle of the night Pop hunting. Margaret, who was our housekeeper back then, would drive me into town and she'd stop in front of the different "establishments," as she called them, while I ran in to see if Pop was there. But that was an occasional thing and I always just saw it as part of my job as older son.

Things took a short turn for the worse right after my mother left, which is a story in itself. Pop had managed to seem pretty much like his old self at the time, but for the next month or two he'd really kept Margaret and me on our toes. I was in the fourth grade then and Ethan was in kindergarten. Mom's leaving didn't come as any big surprise to anybody. She was a good twenty years younger than Pop, and you might say she never really took to family life. She'd packed up and left a couple of different times over the years, but this time somehow Pop and I both knew it was for keeps.

Pop had pulled into the driveway just as Mom and a guy who was *supposed* to be his friend were coming off the front steps and heading for the cab that was waiting to take them to the airport. I figure Margaret must have called Pop at his office to tell him what was happening because it was rare for him to come home midmorning like that. Not only that but he seemed to have arrived ready for business. As easygoing as Pop generally is, he's always had a hop-up-and-down kind of temper when the situation calls for it, and this time he seemed to feel it did. This was understandable since just a few weeks earlier he'd not only gotten this guy off on a felony embezzlement charge but then had offered him an out-of-town place to stay until the publicity died down. When you think about it, the whole deal was pretty raw.

Pop took his time getting out of his car and strolled up to where Mom and the embezzler were coming down the flagstone sidewalk with their suitcases. When he got to them, he took a little more time studying the guy up and down, and then he unloaded a quick right and a quick left into the guy's head. The poor schmo had obviously underestimated Pop, which people who don't know him well enough tend to do, seeing only his modest stature, his gray hair, and his normally sweet disposition, and not knowing it isn't good to get his Irish up. The next thing I knew the schmo was laid out across the front lawn. My mother opened up her compact and took a few seconds to check her makeup one more time, and then said to Pop as if she were asking about the weather, "You don't really think this changes anything, do you?"

"I believe it does!" Pop bellowed, all warmed up now and rocking back on his heels and slurring his words slightly in that way of his which didn't seem to have much to do with whether or not he'd been drinking. "If nothing else, it makes it easier for me to reclaim my shoes!" He then proceeded to pull his Italian cap-toe Oxfords off the make-yourself-at-home and help-yourself-to-it ingrate, who was still flat on his back and staring up at him glassy-eyed.

"I think that's your suit too, Pop," I told him, because it did look like one of his and I always hated to see Pop get the short end of things.

"Good eye, Gabriel, my boy!" Pop rasped out enthusiastically. "I think it might be one of mine at that!" He started yanking the suit off the guy right there on the lawn, handing me the jacket and the vest and then shaking the guy out of the pants—all without bothering to undo any buttons or zippers, so the suit suffered some in the transaction.

A few minutes later as we walked into the house together, Pop, holding his Oxfords in one hand and rubbing my head with his other, told me matter-of-factly, "You know, Gabriel, I'm beginning to think that sonavabitch was guilty after all."

That's the last any of us saw of my mother, or for that matter, the embezzler who got ripped out of the suit, which incidentally, turned out not to be Pop's at all. That was par for the course. Pop always did give me more credit for my abilities than I deserved.

I don't think Pop ever completely got over that day, but it wasn't too long before he'd pulled himself together and things went more or less back to normal. Things took another short turn for the worse a few years later when Margaret died, but Pop managed to pull himself out of that one quicker yet, I think because he realized Margaret's dying had been harder on Ethan and me than our mother's leaving, since Margaret was the one who'd practically raised us.

We never got another full-time housekeeper, but Pop did hire a cook, Jennie, a former student of Bo's mom who came highly recommended by her, and she prepared our evening meals five days a week, Sunday through Thursday, as well as seeing that we had lunches waiting for us on the days following. Fridays and Saturdays we'd eat out, generally at Willie's, which was pretty much the only good restaurant in town. Jennie's job description had gradually grown over the years to take up what she felt was the slack—things like doing dishes, washing clothes, and watering plants—and at the rate we were going, I figured she'd probably be full-time before too long. So all things considered we made out all right. The only thing was, in the past few weeks I'd seen some disturbing signs that Pop might be drifting off again, and that was why I was making a special effort to keep track of him.

The other guys stayed at our camp and Rosasharn and I set out to find Pop. Even though Jeremy had told me that every time he'd turned around in our driveway, the place looked pretty deserted—no lights on, and no Pop's car—I was still hoping to find him home. But he wasn't there, so we headed for town.

I figured if I could catch Pop before he left Willie's, I'd have a pretty good shot at getting him home without too much hassle. Ethan and I had had dinner with him there earlier and he'd seemed in halfway decent spirits at the time. When we'd left to head out to our campsite, he'd stayed on to talk to some friends from Saratoga. I hoped they weren't drinkers. Once Pop got started on the wrong foot, he could be a rip.

Rosasharn and I pulled up in front of Willie's a few minutes later. Rosasharn loved Pop and wanted to go in to say hello, which I wouldn't have minded except he was still in his Green Guy costume. I'd grabbed the headpiece off him as we were pulling into town and I caught a glimpse of him under the first streetlight. I figured his car could attract enough attention on its own. Plus I didn't want to run the risk of having Ray see him looking like that and putting two and two together.

"Thanks, big guy," I said as I got out. "I'll tell Pop you were asking for him."

Rosasharn gave me his Curly wave-off and finessed the clutch for his ferocious-sounding second-gear takeoff.

Pop was on his corner stool at the bar when I walked in. He seemed to be in halfway decent shape, although with Pop it was hard to tell anything was wrong until he was pretty much three sheets to the wind. But just finding him still at Willie's where Charlie could look out for him was a good sign. Charlie was the regular bartender at Willie's, and he had a fine line to walk when it came to keeping Pop on the straight and narrow. If he tried to cut Pop off, or even delivered the drinks too slowly, there was the risk Pop would wander off and go someplace else where he'd be unchaperoned and could get into some real trouble. So whenever Pop seemed up for some serious drinking, Charlie did his level best to keep him there until I came for him, while at the same time trying to keep him as sober as possible for as long as possible. Charlie wasn't much in the personality department, but I really appreciated him for doing that.

"How're ya doing, Pop?" I said, coming up behind him.

Pop turned toward me, his face wrinkling into a melancholy smile. "You know who this guy is?" Pop said, squinting at me, but talking to Charlie.

"I've seen him around," Charlie said, nodding into the big bar mirror at me as he stacked a row of clean glasses.

"Come 'ere and let me have a look at you," Pop

said, even though I couldn't have gotten much closer without climbing onto his lap. That's the way Pop was. He always had to have a look at me. It didn't matter if I'd only been away from him a few hours, or even a few minutes. He was the same way with Ethan.

"I ask you, Charlie," Pop said, wrapping his hand around the back of my neck and studying me with a sad and sleepy kind of awe, "what'd I ever do to deserve a kid like this?" He pulled me in even closer.

Charlie gave me a half smile. He knew the routine.

Pop ruffled my hair and continued. "How's a no-account old codger like myself end up with the kind of boys I have? That's what I'd like to know."

"Somebody made a mistake upstairs," Charlie said.

"You're darn tootin'," Pop told him. "It was a great and wonnerful mistake of cosmic proportions. A *magnificent* cosmic mistake."

"Rosasharn says hello, Pop."

"Rosasharn? He said to say hello, did he?" Pop's wistful smile broke into a wide grin. "Raaahaaa," he rasped out. "Now there's a man after my own heart. That's another wonnerful thing about you, Gabriel. You've got the very best friends in the whole world. The whole world."

"You haven't done so bad there yourself, Pop." It was true. Despite whatever else anybody might say about Pop, you'd be hard pressed to find somebody who didn't like him. Even without all the legal favors he'd done for people over the years, lots of times leaving state senators, and at least one time the Governor of New York himself, waiting while he gave free advice to a neighbor who had a contract problem or a widow worried about protecting her estate from a gambling son-in-law, the fact remained it was hard to know Pop without liking him.

As always, it took a few minutes to get Pop out the door. Pop's the kind of guy who on the way out of a place has to go and shake everybody's hand and say good-bye and find out how everybody's wife and kids are and send them his best. He'd've made a pretty good politician except that he was so sincere. He genuinely *liked* all those people.

We picked up Pop's car at his office just up Main Street, and I dropped Pop and the car off at the house. I was a few months short of sixteen and couldn't drive legally yet even though I was good with a car. Pop taught both Bo and me to drive on the lane that went around Blood Red Pond back when we had to use pillows to see over the dashboard, and when we got a little bigger he let us practice on our road, which was paved but pretty much off the beaten path. Lately Pop seemed content to have me drive him home whenever I was around—even when he was fit to drive himself. We'd met Chief Finnegan a few times, and though he must have known I didn't have a license, he never stopped us. Pop would give him a big friendly wave and say without any intended irony, "Keep up the good work, Michael," in that way Pop had of talking to people who couldn't possibly hear him, being on the other side of two sets of windows. I think the Chief was just as happy to see me driving, license or no license, rather than Pop, who after hours could be a little unpredictable. I never took advantage of his indulgence, driving only when I was picking up Pop and never using the car for my own reasons even if it meant walking or hitching.

Pop was fairly done in after a long day and

seemed content enough to be home. As I was heading down the driveway, he remembered something and came running out on the porch fiddling with the latch on his briefcase. He set the briefcase on one of the porch chairs and pulled something out of it. "From the newsroom," he said, waving it excitedly in the air. "Art just got it in today." He handed me a new Superman comic for Ethan. "And I didn't forget you, Gabriel." He handed me a blue-and-white trade paperback called *Selections from Ralph Waldo Emerson*. I'd mentioned just the other day that we'd read about the American Transcendentalists in English class and how I'd found the whole thing kind of interesting.

"A client picked that up for me in Glens Falls," Pop said, his eyes twinkling. "Now you'll both have something to read around your campfire. And watch out for the bears." For as long as I can remember Pop had joked about bears living in the woods even though no one I knew had ever heard of one being around there. It was just part of our family schtick.

"I don't think any bear in his right mind would try to take on Jeremy and Rosasharn," I told him.

"Raaahaa!" Pop laughed. "You may be right on that account, Gabriel! Give my best to the boys now, will you?"

"Done, Pop." I held up the Emerson book. "And thanks."

"You're most welcome," Pop said. "Always welcome. Enjoy." He was still waving when I got to the road.

Three

I woke up with dew on my head and remembered all of a sudden that I *really* hate to camp. It wasn't just my damp head, or the general feeling of dampness that extended down into my sleeping bag. *Or* the fact that I could almost see my breath. *Or* the rocky ground I could feel bruising my shoulder blades. But put all this together, and then add the fact that we all had real beds waiting for us at home, and temperature-controlled rooms, and bathrooms with hot showers, and you have to wonder what we were all doing sleeping out on the range.

I made a mental note of all this, hoping it might save me from ever waking up in that condition again, and then sat up and looked around. Bo was already meditating, something he'd been doing twice a day every day since he was a little kid. Bo's whole family meditated, even his little sister, who was only nine. She did some kind of a kid's version, where you meditate while you're on the go—brushing your teeth, making your bed, that kind of thing. I remember Bo doing it when we were her age.

I pulled the sleeping bag tighter around my neck and watched him for a minute. He sat there in full lotus, eyes closed and wearing a blank peaceful look. He wasn't completely still like they always show people meditating in movies or on TV. Sometimes his head would roll around in a circle working kinks out of his neck, and sometimes his whole body would start to rock as if he were in a car going over bumps. I'm sure the entire deal would have looked pretty strange if you hadn't grown up around it, but I had. Besides, when it came to Bo's family, the meditation part of the program was only the beginning if you want to talk about unusual. But we'll get to that later.

Just then Bo started to stretch a little, which usually meant he was about done, and within a few minutes he opened his eyes and got to his feet. He stood there a second looking back through a clearing where you could see the beginning of an orange glow on the eastern horizon. I climbed out of my sleeping bag, wrapped it around my shoulders, and trudged up beside him to watch as the glow expanded.

"Well, guys," Bo said finally, "is this great or what?"

It wasn't till then that I looked down and saw that Ethan was standing beside me, all wrapped up in his sleeping bag the same way I was.

"I still hate camping," I told them, but had to admit to myself this was pretty decent. The top third of the sun was showing now, and you could almost see it climbing. Ethan stayed quiet, which was pretty much how he stayed most of the time, but mornings, forget it—I hardly ever heard Ethan's voice before ten o'clock. His eyes were wide, though, and his jaw was dropped down, so I knew he was enjoying the whole thing too. We kept watching until the sun was above the horizon and moving up through some tree branches.

"Impressive or what?" Bo asked, cocking an eyebrow.

"Not bad," I said. "What do you do for an encore?"

"Be here tonight and I'll set her back down for you," he told me, smiling. "Right over there." He waved his arm west over our campsite, where Jeremy and

Rosasharn were still sacked out—Jeremy tucked way down inside his sleeping bag and probably scowling, and Rosasharn on his back, eyes closed but his mouth already smiling up at the new day.

"Try not to land it near Jeremy if you want it to come again," I told him.

The sleeping bag containing Jeremy moved a little, so I figured he was awake and listening to us.

"Hey, Ethan," I said. "Is that a snake over there by Jeremy?"

Ethan gave a little smile and nodded. He knew the routine. For years I'd driven Jeremy crazy by pointing at the ground under his feet and saying, "Snake!" because it was so much fun to watch him dance. A few times there really *had* been a snake there, so Jeremy could never be sure if I was putting him on or not.

"Shuddup," the sleeping bag told me.

"I think it's one of those timber rattlers, Ethe. Remember how they caught a couple of those around Lake George last summer?"

Ethan nodded again. The sleeping bag said to shut up again.

Rosasharn's eyes were open now and his smile was bigger than ever. He slipped the rest of the way out of his sleeping bag and started tiptoeing toward Jeremy. When he was almost there, Jeremy's sleeping bag sat up and Jeremy's scowly head popped out the top.

"Don't even start, ya tub," the head told him.

Pop was up and all set to cook a big breakfast for us when Ethan and I walked in.

"Aaah," Pop said, breaking into a smile when he saw us, "our modern-day Daniel Boones have returned from the wilderness." First he pulled us both into him and gave a squeeze, and then he leaned back to get a good look at us.

"I'm no Daniel Boone, Pop," I told him. "If he'd been like me, we'd still be waiting for somebody to discover Kentucky."

Pop laughed. "Notwithstanding the native population's claim to that distinction."

"They're another reason I'd've passed on Kentucky," I said, grabbing my hair and miming a scalp removal.

"Raaah," Pop laughed, rocking back on his heels. "Billy admits they used to trim a little close," he said. "But they didn't charge anything for the service, so how could you make a case against them?" He let loose another laugh at that one. Billy was William Whitecloud. He and Pop had become friends years earlier when Pop represented his tribe in a land-claim action in the Adirondacks. I remember the first time Mr. Whitecloud and his wife came to dinner at our house. Pop, never being one to walk on eggshells, had opened the door for them and yelled back to us, "Indians, boys! Quick, circle the automobiles!" Without batting an eye, Mr. Whitecloud responded in an old Hollywood Indian accent, "Come for Irish seven-course dinner—six-pack and heap-big potato." Pop loved it. He bear-hugged both of them and must have kept laughing for five minutes.

Humor and affection went hand in hand with Pop, and I think he believed that to leave somebody out of a joke was another way of saying you didn't feel entirely comfortable with him. Some of Pop's best stories were about the Irish, and his favorite one fell out of our own family tree. It concerned his grandfather, whom he never knew due to a job-related mishap that took place when Pop's mother was still a little girl. The way the story goes, our dear departed great granddad somehow managed to fall headfirst into an open vat of beer at the South Troy brewery where he worked, and died a few days later of complications resulting from breathing in the toxic gases. This part is family history and no one disputes it. Many of the relatives do dispute Pop's version, though, which holds that upon being pulled from the vat, the guy punched and wrestled himself free and then hopped back in. They also deny another of Pop's claims—that he was buried with a gigantic smile on his face.

"At any rate," Pop said, running a hand through my unscalped scalp, "you look good to me just the way you are." Then he ran a hand through Ethan's hair. "And we wouldn't want to change anything on you now either, would we, Ethan?"

"Gabe told Jeremy there was a rattlesnake near his sleeping bag," Ethan said proudly.

"I'm sure Jeremy was delighted to receive *that* piece of information," Pop said, smiling and rubbing Ethan's head some more.

Ethan laughed. "He was mad," he said.

"Raaah, raah!" Pop roared. "Yes, I'll bet he was at that."

Pop then led us into the kitchen and made us his Saturday morning specialty, what he called his world-famous, Tex-Mex-style western omelet. Between Jennie's cooking during the week, and the things Pop made or brought home on the weekends, it's a wonder Ethan and I weren't real tub scouts, but we were anything but. Pop was lean as a post too, but then he didn't eat the way we did, or at least not the way I did. Not even close.

Back in my room, after a long, leisurely shower where I tried to wash the lingering dampness of the great outdoors away, I went to grab my favorite pair of jeans. The only thing was they weren't there. I knew for a fact they'd been in a pile of clean clothes Jennie had folded and left on the stairs a few days earlier, along with my gray Key West henley and some socks and underwear and things. I almost remembered carrying the pile up to my room, but that didn't mean much. I almost remembered doing a lot of things I never did. I padded out to the hall and checked the stairs. No luck. Next I checked Ethan's room, and then Pop's, in case my things had somehow gotten mixed in with theirs. No luck there either. None of this surprised me. I sometimes think I spend half my life looking for things I've been busy losing during the other half. It was no big deal. My missing stuff generally turned up on its own when it was good and ready, so I never got too bent out of shape unless it was something I absolutely needed that minute, which I didn't this time. I threw on another pair of jeans and then dug out an old green-and-white rugby shirt.

I was eager to get back to the Emerson book Pop had bought me. I'd managed to read a little of it around the campfire the night before. Jeremy, after studying me like a hawk, had announced I'd better not be going off on another of my kicks and driving everybody crazy. I responded by throwing a marshmallow at him, even though I'm the first to admit I do go off the deep end from time to time. A few years earlier I went through a phase where I tried to convince everybody that Brian Wilson was an underrated musical genius. It didn't stop me that no one else my age even knew who Brian Wilson was—or cared. I'd learned about him from a documentary on the Disney Channel and decided everyone else should know about him too.

After that played itself out, I spent two solid months studying old racing forms that Art saved me from the newsroom, trying to design a system I could use to beat the races that summer at Saratoga. What I ended up with worked great on paper, netting me a hypothetical fortune on horses I picked from already-run races at Belmont. Unfortunately the first two times I actually went to the track I ended up losing almost a hundred dollars. (Jeremy lost fifty, which had the effect of further dampening his enthusiasm for my hobbies.)

Then I went through my magic phase, where I pored over about twenty different books on famous magicians and escape artists, trying to learn everything I could about how they were able to do all the things they did. I learned a few tricks, but before I got anywhere near good my mind had already graduated to something else.

What happened was, the whole idea of creating illusions got me thinking more about reality itself. Because if things can *seem* so real and not be, you have to start wondering what *is* real, and when you start getting into that, you find out that most of the things around you are a lot less real than you thought.

I know that sounds far-fetched when you first hear it, but the more you think about it, the more sense it makes. Take, say, something like a hunk of wood. On the surface level the wood is real enough, and if somebody were to hit you over the head with it, it wouldn't do you a whole lot of good. But if you trace the makeup of that hunk of wood beyond its molecules and get to the atomic level, you find that what's actually there is just a bunch of electrons whirling around submicroscopic nuclei—kind of like miniature solar systems consisting mostly of empty space. And here's where it really starts to hit you. The electrons aren't *things* at all—not solid physical things anyway. They're just energy. So you're left with nothing solid but the nuclei. And if you study *them,* the little neutrons and protons, it turns out these little guys are nothing but waves of energy too. So you start with a solid, hurt-your-head-with-it hunk of wood, and in the end you find out it's nothing but an expression of some kind of energy soup. And this is true of everything you see around you, from a banana peel to somebody's mother-in-law.

That's one of the things that struck me as I'd plunged into the Emerson book that morning. He seemed to know this stuff back when scientists hadn't even discovered *bacteria,* let alone the atom. He learned it from studying the ancient Indian holy books. I kept rereading the second stanza of his poem "Brahma," which is what the Hindus call the soul of the universe:

> Far or forget to me is near;
> Shadow and sunlight are the same;
> The vanished gods to me appear;
> And one to me are shame and fame.

What he seemed to be saying was, everything is actually *one* thing—even things that appear to be opposites. And when you see that underlying unity, I guess he was saying you see God. Bo and I'd had plenty of late-night and all-night discussions about this kind of thing—Bo being kind of Eastern in his approach to life, as you might guess—so this wasn't completely new to me. I thought about it some more and then read the poem through to the end. The next stanza was trickier, and I was wishing Bo was there so I could run it by him.

> They reckon ill who leave me out;
> When me they fly, I am the wings;
> I am the doubter and the doubt,
> And I the hymn the Brahmin sings.

I checked my dictionary and found that the Brahmins were the priestly class in India, but I still couldn't get the whole thing to come together for me. I read it over two or three more times, still not quite getting all of it, but liking it anyway. Whenever I hit that stanza, I'd smile, thinking about how Ethan would love the part about flying.

And for the time being at least, I'd pretty much forgotten about the missing clothes.

Four

Bo called from the country club around noon. He'd turned sixteen in the spring and gotten a job in the pro shop, where he handed out people's clubs when they went out to play and then cleaned them and put them away when they were done. In between, he worked the cash register when the pro was out giving a lesson or having lunch. The hours weren't bad and neither were the tips. Anyway, he'd be getting out at three and wondered if I wanted to do anything. I told him to swing by and we'd come up with something.

Pop was at his office, which is pretty usual for him on a Saturday, always having more of a workload than he can take care of in a five-day week. Ethan had taken his Holstein calf out of our little barn and was in the front yard trying to halter-train it. Pop had given him the calf for Christmas, and Ethan was planning to show it at the county fair at the end of the summer. I'd been showing cattle at the fair each year since I was Ethan's age and had gone on to state fair twice. All the calves I'd raised were over at Jeremy's farm now, having grown into cows and needing to be milked twice a day, which didn't always fit into my schedule, especially after the novelty wore off. I wasn't sure if I was going to show them this year or not. Not only is it a lot of work, but when you're almost sixteen, you're supposed to be too cool for that kind of thing. I knew I'd probably end up doing it, though, partly for Ethan's sake, and partly because I actually still got a kick out of it.

I felt bad when I looked out and saw Ethan gently tugging on his calf all by himself. When I was training my three calves to lead, Ethan was with me every minute, getting behind them and pushing when they got stubborn, even though at the time they were a lot bigger than he was. Ethan probably wanted me to help him, but if he knows I'm in my room reading or doing homework or even taking a nap, he'll never disturb me. I never told him not to bother me or yelled at him for it or anything like that. It's just the way Ethan's always been. When he was younger, sometimes I'd find him outside my room, just sitting there in the hall, waiting for me to come out. As he got older, he wouldn't sit and wait for me anymore. He'd start doing whatever it was he wanted to do by himself, but always close by so I could join him when I was ready. I try to remember him, but he's so quiet and it's easy for me to get all wrapped up in what I'm doing and forget he's even there. I've told him a million times to let me know when he wants me for something, but he never will.

"How about I give her a push, Ethe?" I said from the porch.

He nodded, the earnest look on his face brightening into a smile.

I jumped off the porch and leaned into the back of his calf the way he used to do with mine. Ethan gave another little pull from his end, and the calf took a reluctant, stumbling step before planting her feet even more solidly.

"Cappy can be stubborn," Ethan told me. "Can't you, Cappy?" He stopped tugging and rubbed her forehead. Cappy's full name was Sugar Hill Titan's

Capricorn. Most registered cattle have important-sounding names like that. Sugar Hill was the name of the Wulfsons' farm, which is where Cappy came from, Titan was from the sire's name, and the Capricorn part was all hers.

We spent the next hour or so pushing and pulling Cappy around the yard, but the lesson didn't seem to be taking. The odd thing was that if Ethan dropped the halter, she'd follow him anyplace he went, but that wasn't good enough. When he got Cappy into the ring, he'd have to grip the halter right next to her chin and hold her head up just so, and be able to have her take half a step forward or backward if that's what the judge wanted. Of course, that's all theoretical. I'd seen plenty of kids get dragged into or out of the ring by their animals, and it had even happened to me a few times.

"What if she won't learn?" Ethan said at one point, looking up at me.

"She will," I said. "As much as any of them do. Remember what June did to me the first year I showed her, Ethe?"

Ethan looked at me and shook his head. He'd been pretty young then. June had been a full-grown cow for a couple of years and this happened when she was still a junior heifer calf, which is the youngest division there is.

"I led her into the ring," I told him, "and everything was going fine. Then just before the judge came over to look at her, she decided to lie down in the sawdust right where she was. She just lay there chewing her cud and looking around at all the people in the stands. No matter what I did she wouldn't budge. Then the kid behind me tried to help by pushing on her. Then the judge himself got into the act. Don't you remember that, Ethan? Pop got such a charge out of the whole thing. I could hear him roaring from the stands on the other side of the ring."

Ethan gave a quiet little smile, and I could see his face was brighter and the story'd had an effect on him. Ethan's funny; he'll worry about all kinds of things, but as soon as he finds out that something he's been worried about has already happened to me or Pop or even Bo, then he'll stop worrying about it. It's as if he thinks, if it happened to us, it must be all right.

He was still looking happy when we finished up and walked in from the barn. "Pop really got a charge out of it, huh?" he said, smiling up at me.

"Yeah," I told him. "He really did."

Not long after that Bo pulled up in The Tank. The Tank was actually a late-model, top-of-the-line Lexus, but it had earned that name because of Bo's father's history of using it to drive through things. Actually, this was the third in a series of Tanks. The original Tank had been dubbed by us about six years earlier when Mr. Michaelson had used it to put a new opening in the back of their two-car garage. It seems he got a story idea just as he was pulling into the driveway and was jotting it down after he parked in the garage. Unfortunately he never got around to taking the car out of drive, and it was creeping forward the whole time he was scribbling down the idea. When he heard the first telltale crunching sounds, he went for the brake but caught the gas instead and ended up on the back lawn. The thing that got me was he sat there for a few minutes getting the rest of the idea down before he climbed out to check damages. I still kind of admire him for that.

"Do I see a new dent?" I said as Bo got out.

"Good eye," he said. "Dad had a run-in yesterday with one of those mail collection boxes on Main Street."

"Whose fault?" I said with a straight face.

Bo had Ethan in a headlock and was pretending to whale on him. "Hard to say," he said, deadpan. "They never found the guy driving the mailbox."

It's not that Mr. M. wasn't a good driver; he was actually pretty handy behind the wheel. It's just that too many times his *body* was behind the wheel and his mind wasn't. Bo explained it away by saying his father had no earth signs. He wrote books for a living, so spacing out was right up his alley. Anyway, every Christmas Mr. M. would send fruit baskets and signed books to anybody whose car he'd hit or whose property he'd damaged. The list grew a little larger each year. I was even on it. He'd backed over my bicycle when I was ten.

We decided to head over to Bo's house and review the footage we'd gotten the night before. First we dropped Ethan off at Pop's office. At the end of each week Ethan liked to hang around there and help Pop organize everything, which, unlike me, he was amazingly good at. Pop said lots of times Ethan was able to find files that even his secretary hadn't been able to locate. Nothing against Pop's secretary; it's just that when it comes to misplacing things, Pop is right up there in my league.

"Let's check out Rosa's first," I said as we pulled away from in front of Pop's office. Rosa's was, among other things, the tavern on the outskirts of town that was run by Rosasharn's family. They also made the best pizza around—take-out mostly, but they did have a small dining room right off the kitchen. Rosasharn's parents were real entrepreneur types and were always looking for ways to expand their operation. A few years ago they added a little laundromat, and last year they opened a ten-unit motel. This year they were planning on putting up a row of those self-storage sheds that people could rent. The place had already grown into a hodgepodge of buildings that some of the locals referred to facetiously as "the mall."

Another thing—Rosa's just happened to be where Ray McPherson and his crew generally landed on Saturday afternoons, and I was eager to hear what kind of stories, if any, Ray was telling about his aborted trip down our road the other night.

Rosasharn and Sudie were in the kitchen making pizzas when we walked in. Jeremy was there too. They had him grating cheese, and he was busy scowling down at the little pile he'd just made.

"So how's our charred buddy doing?" Bo said, meaning Rosasharn.

"Excellentay, o maestro of film," Rosasharn said, bowing. "Most excellentay."

"Most stupiday," Jeremy said, and then held up the cheese grater in a blocking action because whenever he said anything that sounded even remotely French, Rosasharn would pretend to be Gomez Addams and try to kiss his way up Jeremy's arm.

"I love it when you speak French, Morticia," Rosasharn said to the cheese grater.

"I leave this guy alone for one night," Sudie said, "and he almost burns himself up." She drew her arm back as if she were about to give Rosasharn a good backhand.

"Did he tell you what else he did?" I asked her.

She nodded and tried to aim a look of scorn his way. She couldn't keep a smile from breaking through, though, so she drew her arm back and actually swatted him this time. "Ya goof," she said.

"I must protect zee swamp," Rosasharn said.

"Has Ray been in yet?" I asked.

Rosasharn turned and pointed like a bird dog to the door behind him, which led to the bar.

Sudie rolled her eyes. "He got here an hour ago and he's already been through the story at least three times. The last time he told it, the thing practically tried to yank him out of his car."

"You didn't tell him it was Rosasharn, did you?" I said, remembering Ray's crazy side.

Sudie shook her head. "Why spoil his fun? Speaking of which, Clutzy Lutzy just pulled in before you guys, so Ray's probably going through the whole nine yards again."

This we had to hear. We filed into the bar and headed for the pool table, which Mr. Rosa let us use afternoons. I started racking the balls, but quietly so I wouldn't miss any of the story.

Ray was at the bar, front and center, already zeroed in on Harold Lutz, also known as Clutzy Lutzy— a name he'd picked up because league night for him doubled as drinking night, and he had a tendency to fall on his face at least once while bowling his last frames. Ray was punctuating his point with a Budweiser bottle aimed at Clutzy's chest.

"You can laugh if you want," he said, "but I'm telling you it happened."

Clutzy squinted at him. "I ain't laughing," he said. "You're forgettin'. I seen a ghost for myself that time. I seen it with my own eyes."

We all knew *that* story. Years ago Clutz had been fixing up the Briggs place a mile east of town, and one day he heard footsteps downstairs. Thinking it was his wife bringing his lunch, he yelled that he was upstairs and then went back to ripping out the old lathing and plaster. The footsteps kept coming his way but nobody said anything. As Clutzy told it, in thirty years he'd never known Ellie to keep her mouth shut when there was a working set of ears within range, so he became suspicious and walked over to the door. That's when he saw his ghost heading right toward him. He swears it was old Mr. Briggs himself, a crotchety old miser who'd checked out weeks earlier as the result of a blast from his own shotgun. The death was ruled accidental, but Clutz has since developed a foul-play theory which he says would explain why Old Man Briggs was trying to make contact with him. Anyway, the ghost kept coming right at him, not saying anything, and not picking up any speed but not slowing down any either. When it came into the room with him, Clutzy decided he was feeling a little crowded and left through the handiest exit, which happened to be the window behind him. As you might imagine, he took a lot of ribbing for that story over the years, but he still swore by it, defending his ghost diagnosis by explaining how he could see the thing and see right through it at the same time, and adding that he wouldn't have jumped out any second-story window if he hadn't been absolutely sure of the facts.

"I don't wanna hear that friggin' ghost story again," Ray said, obviously not feeling any kind of supernatural kinship with Clutz. "I'm not talkin' about sonavabitchin' Casper here! What I seen was a real live two-dimensional *thing*, for chrissake! It was bouncing the front of my friggin' car up and down, and there ain't no ghost can do that."

41

"Well, whaddaya think it was?" Clutzy wanted to know.

"I don't know," Ray said, shaking his head. "But I'll tell you one thing. . . ." He took a dramatic sip from his Budweiser before continuing. "Whatever it was, it wasn't human."

"I coulda told him that," Jeremy mumbled from behind me.

"And whatever it was," Ray continued, "the son-avabitch wasn't alone. Right before *it* come after me, I seen something else on that friggin' road. It come out from behind Old Man Lindstrom's barn and scooted across in front of me. I slowed down to try to get a look at whatever the hell *that* was when—bam!—this other ugly-assed thing jumps in front of me. I'm tellin' ya, there's something to all them stories about that place. Laugh if you want, but that thing on my hood was as friggin' real as you are."

"I ain't laughing," Clutzy said solemnly. "I'm the one who's seen a ghost myself."

"Shut your ass about your sonavabitchin' ghost. What I seen was no friggin' ghost."

I could feel a pain starting to develop in my side from trying to hold it in. I figured Bo and Jeremy must've been in about the same boat. Then all of a sudden a thought struck me. Ray had said he'd seen something else besides Rosasharn that night. And right across the road from Mr. Lindstrom's barn—exactly where I'd seen Ethan staring right after Ray had made his getaway. If I hadn't seen the look on Ethan's face, I'd've thought Ray was the biggest liar in the world for sure. As it was, I just didn't know.

Five

I'm a big fan of Sundays. Days off, in general, I'm all in favor of, but Sunday, being my second free day in a row, is when I'm just hitting my stride at being laid-back. We'd taken care of mass on Saturday evening before dinner, so I didn't even have to deal with sitting there thinking that every time Father Ryan looked my way he was having visions of Sister Violet and the *Rogue Nun* stampede.

Ethan and I started the day with our usual seven-mile run, making a big circle that took us into town and out the other side, and then doubling around past the Wulfsons' farm and, after a few more turns, back onto our road from the other end. I never pushed for time on Sunday, considering it more of a family outing than training, but even so, I could see that Ethan was turning into a pretty fair runner. He loped alongside me with long easy strides and, as far as I could tell, never once had to breathe through his mouth. And this was a kid who didn't even train. Just out of curiosity I picked up the pace for the last half mile or so and Ethan didn't lose a foot of ground. We hit the driveway, neck and neck, at pretty close to a full sprint.

"You'll be leaving me in the dust one of these days, Ethe," I said as we climbed the porch steps.

"No I won't," he said, giving his little smile. I don't think he meant it to be modest. I think he just meant he liked running with me so why would he want to go out ahead.

After we'd showered and dressed and had Sunday brunch, courtesy of Pop, I decided to ride my bike over to Bo's and see what was doing over there. He'd had a date with Gretchen Chambers the night before, and I'd stayed home and watched a movie with Ethan and Pop. I enjoyed doing it and have no complaints, but I've never been one who could stay put too long without getting a little stir-crazy. Pop says I have the roving spirit of the Irish in me.

It was pushing noon when I left. Pop and Ethan were involved in another of their big chess tournaments, and Pop was fighting him off with all he had. I remembered how it wasn't so long ago that Pop would have to sandbag so that Ethan could win once in a while, but now he couldn't even get away with any philosophizing or telling stories during their games because by the time he came out the other end of his spiel, Ethan would have put him away. Pop would raise a fuss whenever he lost, vowing a concentration unrivaled in Western civilization for their next match, but he didn't fool me. I knew how much he loved seeing Ethan win.

When I got to Bo's, he was in the living room watching an old *Flipper* episode on The Family Channel. You might think that a future-valedictorian type like Bo would avoid TV like the plague, or that he'd only watch PBS or Arts & Entertainment, but it wasn't the case. He loved all those old shows—including the cornball animal rescue things. He also loved the classic TV Westerns like *Bonanza* and *Gunsmoke* and *The Rifleman.* My personal favorite was *F Troop,* but that may have been the result of watching it one time with Pop and Mr. Whitecloud, who both practically fell off the couch laughing every time they showed the Hekawi

Indians and their stone-faced, wheeling-and-dealing chief.

Bo's little sister Erika was lying on the floor in front of him, drawing in her sketchbook and being Bo's footrest. When she saw me her face lit up and she slid out from under Bo's feet. "I'm making you something, Gabe," she said, and reached for her drawing tablet. "See? It's you!" She sat up and handed it to me.

I took the thing in my hands and stared down at it. She didn't need to say it was me; it *was* me. It was incredible and it would have been incredible even if she hadn't been only nine years old. Erika didn't work in crayon like most kids her age, but did mostly pencil sketches and occasional watercolors. This was a pencil sketch, and she'd nailed me. She'd captured both my trademarks—the first being my hair, which except for the color (Pop's was gray and mine was brown) was exactly like Pop's, longish and wavy, bordering on wild (Pop called it free-spirited), and the second being my slightly cockeyed smile. I don't know where that came from, but I'd always had a way of smiling out of one side of my mouth, and it made me look a little like a wise guy, although I don't think I am particularly. Pop always told me I had the face of a choirboy who was thinking seriously of defecting, which was probably as good a way of putting it as any. I stared down at the picture, amazed. Being unable myself to draw much more than stick men with captions coming out of their mouths, it always gets me how, with just a few lines, some people can capture whatever it is that makes a person distinctive. *Especially* when the one doing the drawing is a kid.

"Wow," I said, still studying the picture as I handed it back to her, "that's really great." Which wasn't nearly enough to say how I really felt. I mean, I wasn't fighting back a river of tears or anything like that, but I was touched. I really was. Just the thought of her pouring herself into that picture for my benefit got to me, and I would've hugged her if I were the hugging type.

Erika smiled and slid the sketchbook back in front of her. Bo's feet were draped over her shoulders now and sticking out on either side of her head. She didn't mind. She put that earnest look back on her face, the one that almost all little kids get when they're all wrapped up in something, and went back to drawing. I watched her for a minute, and then plopped down next to Bo on the couch just as the show broke for a commercial. "So how's Flipper doing today?" I asked him.

"Couldn't be better," Bo said. "He sends his regards."

"You know," I said, stretching out and slumping into my usual couch posture, "the thing that gets me about *Flipper* is that the kids never get into any life-threatening situations unless they're in the water—or at least close enough to it so Flipper can point out the situation to a responsible adult. It doesn't make sense."

Bo looked at me. "They're not allowed to go inland," he said. "With their track record, it'd just be too risky."

"What about school?" I asked. "Haircuts? The dentist?"

Bo shook his head. "Nope. Not unless they're within Flipper range."

Erika had gone back to lying on the floor and was now working away with *two* sets of feet resting on her. She scrunched her head around and studied us as we discussed the behind-the-scenes rules governing life in Flipperville. She was never quite sure just how seriously she should take most of our conversations.

Right then the front door opened and Mr. and Mrs. Michaelson walked in. They were wearing their tennis things and carrying rackets so it was easy to see what they'd been up to. As they walked into the living room Flipper was jumping around in the water making that annoying noise he makes. Practically every *Flipper* episode ends the same way. Everybody stands around the water and one of them delivers a lame joke about how lucky they are to have Flipper around to save the day while he shows off by doing flips and tailstands. This never fails to crack up the whole cast.

"Another triumphant denouement?" Mrs. Michaelson said, being possibly the only human on the planet who would refer to the ending of a *Flipper* episode as a denouement.

Mr. and Mrs. Michaelson almost single-handedly proved the theory that opposites attract. Mr. M. wrote books for kids—kids Ethan's age and younger—sometimes novels, sometimes picture books, anything from mysteries to humor and fantasy, and he was even talking about trying his hand at science fiction. Go into any bookstore or library in the country and you're bound to see some titles by Lawrence Michaelson. I always considered him a genius in his own way, but there was no denying he was a kid at heart, and he loved those old TV shows as much as Bo did. Mrs. M., on the other hand, didn't even watch TV. A lot of people make a big deal out of slipping it into conversations how they don't watch TV, but Mrs. M. really *didn't* watch it—ever, except for documentaries or an occasional film (usually with subtitles). For her, the theme to *The Lone Ranger* was, and would always be, the "William Tell Overture." That wasn't their only difference. She was formal; he was casual. She was meticulous; he was absentminded. I could go on and on.

About the only thing the Michaelsons were in perfect sync on was their meditation program, which they did together twice a day. I say meditation *program* because they didn't just meditate. They were also flyers. The actual Transcendental Meditation term for what they were was "sidhas," but "flyers" captured the flavor of the whole thing, and even TMers use the word. It meant they'd been trained in the yoga sutras of an ancient and revered mystic named Patanjali. I'm no expert on Patanjali himself, but I do know that the yoga sutras are what you might call a set of mental formulas for achieving supernormal functioning—one of the most dramatic of those functions being levitation. Bo had heard that there were at least a few people in India who were actually levitating, but pretty much everybody else (the other sidhas) spent their levitating time hopping around on foam rubber in the lotus position, working on developing their minds to the point where they'd eventually lift up and *stay* up. I'm not sure if I really believe that will ever happen, but I have to admit I kind of like the idea of it.

Because I grew up with it, I never found the notion of people flying all that bizarre. I'd always listened to Bo telling stories about Indian holy men doing this or that extraordinary thing, and I'd read *Autobiography of a Yogi* when I was twelve. That book is filled with stories of people doing miraculous things, including St. Joseph of Cupertino, who couldn't even take his turn serving the other monks at their meals because of his tendency to float to the ceiling, dishes and all, whenever he had a particularly happy thought. Then there was St. Teresa of Avila, who supposedly used to lift off regularly, whether she planned on it or not. I remember reading the whole section on levitation to Ethan a few years ago, and of course he thought it was the greatest thing in the world, feeling the way he did about flying. He's always been crazy about anything that had to do with flying. When he was seven or eight, for his birthday Bo made him a painting he called *The Second Flight of Icarus,* which was based on the Brueghel painting *The Fall of Icarus.*

In case you don't remember, Icarus and his father, Daedalus, tried to escape the island they'd been imprisoned on by making wings out of feathers and wax. The wings worked like a charm, and it looked as if they might pull it off until Icarus got a little carried away and flew too close to the sun, which unfortunately melted the wax on his wings and sent him into a major nosedive. In the Brueghel painting, all you see of Icarus are his legs sticking out of the water after taking the Nestea plunge. In the forefront of the painting is a plowman who's plodding along behind his horse and plow. His head is down, and you get the feeling he's never in his life lifted his eyes to the sky—the sky where Icarus has just been.

Bo's painting uses pretty much the same setting, but in his, Icarus is still high in the air, stretched full out and soaring for all he's worth, a look of joyful serenity on his face. And he doesn't have to worry about his wings melting, because he's not wearing any. In some way that I can't quite describe he has this quality of lightness about him, and you never for a minute think he's going to fall. Below him is the plowman, so solid and dense-looking I always had the sense that he was actually sinking into the ground. Even when you look at it close-up, it's hard to tell where the guy's boots leave off and the dirt begins. I always felt a little sad when I looked at that plowman. Something about the way he was trudging along behind the horse reminded me of Mr. Lindstrom and the way he plodded around on his land. Ethan loved the painting, though, and since the day he got the thing, he's had it hanging on the wall at the foot of his bed where he can see it first thing in the morning and last thing at night.

"Remember when we were kids, hon?" Mr. M. said from the hall closet, where he was dumping the tennis rackets. "And all the Westerns we used to watch?"

"I remember when we were kids," she said, reaching in and straightening up the rackets, "but I don't remember the Westerns."

"My favorite was *Fury*," Mr. M. continued wistfully. "My brothers and I watched that show every Saturday morning, no matter what. Remember *Fury*, hon?"

"I'm afraid I don't, dear."

"*Hon*," he said, miming disbelief. "Don't toy with me here. You couldn't have gone all the way through your childhood without watching *Fury*." He followed her over toward the stairs. "You remember—he was a horse, a shiny black horse, and he saved Joey every week."

"Sorry, dear. You know that's not my forte." She pronounced it "fort," not "fortay," which is how most people say it, and a little smugly too because it sounds foreign, not having a clue they're using the wrong word. I'd learned all those pronunciation subtleties from Mrs. M. over the years. You could say correct pronunciation was her forte.

"But how could you have missed *Fury*?" Mr. M. said, scratching his head in disbelief as she headed up the stairs. He shot a mischievous smile our way and then looked back up at her. "Do you suppose maybe they didn't get that show on your planet?" he asked her.

"That may explain it, dear," we heard from the top of the stairs.

Bo had to work the pro shop starting at three, so he dropped me and my bicycle off at my house on the way. I figured since Ethan and Pop would most likely be done with their chess tournament by then, Ethan might want to go out for a hike. We were both big on hiking, or exploring anyway, and it seemed like a perfect afternoon for that kind of thing. Plus, Pop liked to get in a Sunday afternoon nap whenever he could, and I wanted to make sure that this week he could. I wondered if part of his problem in the last few weeks hadn't been just a matter of his not having enough time to call his own. I was well aware of the fact that for years Pop had worked hard at being father, mother, and breadwinner for us. After a while that kind of pressure has to take its toll.

As we headed out, Ethan said he hoped we could find the family of beavers that used to live on the swamp side of Blood Red Pond up until a couple of years ago. One day we'd gone over there to watch them, and they were gone. Mr. Lindstrom told us that was the way beavers were, that they'd stay in one spot for a while and chomp down all kinds of saplings for their lodge, and when they used up the ones they wanted, they moved on.

Ethan and I had spent a lot of time hiking along the many no-name streams that eventually feed into the Hudson River a few miles west of our place. We'd never found so much as a single beaver, but Ethan didn't seem to mind. He got a kick out of just being out there looking. Ethan was a lot like Bo in that regard, having that ability to just enjoy things without having to have them come out exactly how he planned them. If I live long enough, I may get that way myself.

In keeping with tradition, we didn't find any beavers that day either, but we did find an old house foundation way out in the middle of the woods, and we explored around in there for a while. We wondered about the people who'd lived there—what they'd been like, what happened to them, and if we knew their grandchildren or great-grandchildren, that kind of thing. What got me was, I knew that the people who'd lived in this old place had been every bit as real as *we* were, and I tried to imagine our house like that, disintegrated down to the foundation, overrun by trees and vines and totally forgotten. It kind of gave me the creeps to think about it. I don't adjust that well to change—even if it hasn't happened yet.

As we were walking home that evening, I saw Ethan give a little wave—what Bo and I always called his aloha wave because it was the same whether he was coming or going. I looked way across the field we were in front of to see Mr. Lindstrom wave back at us. He had good eyes for an old guy, and didn't miss much when it came to anything going on around his land. You wouldn't even know he was looking at you, but if you waved at him—even Ethan's shy little wave—he'd wave back. At least he would to us. If he didn't know you, or knew you and didn't like you, you could end up with a different kind of gesture entirely.

I don't remember if I waved to him that day or not. I may just have let Ethan's wave do the job for both of us. Not that it made much difference at the time. I had no idea then that it would be the last time I'd ever see Mr. Lindstrom out and around like that.

Six

On Monday morning Pop dropped Ethan off at the middle school and then pulled around to let me off at the high school. "Give 'em hell, Gabe," he told me, and roared out a laugh. He'd said the same thing to Ethan, and it was pretty much the same thing he said to both of us every day. He didn't mean anything by it; neither of us gave much hell to anybody as a rule. It was just Pop's way of saying good-bye.

"You give 'em hell too, Pop," I said as I got out of the car.

"I fully intend to, Gabriel. I fully intend to."

In Pop's case he probably would—or at least I hoped he would. He was on his way to the courthouse in Hudson Falls, where he was defending a guy accused of poisoning his ex-girlfriend's cat—an unpopular side to be on since nobody likes cat poisoners. To make things worse, all the TV stations and newspapers were jockeying for the easy moral high ground, which Pop says is often a simple matter of supplying the public with somebody convenient to hate. They kept showing videos of the cat during its happier moments, then of the girlfriend crying and holding its little cat corpse. Pop figured he'd have to fight tooth and nail to keep the focus on the real issue of the trial: whether the guy was actually guilty, which in Pop's mind was somewhat doubtful since at least one person who knew them insisted it was the *guy* who'd broken it off with the girl and she'd been pretty angry about the whole thing. And this supposedly happened right before the poisoning took place. But that didn't stop the animal lovers. Every night on the evening news you'd see them out in front of the courthouse, their faces twisted in anger, demanding justice. Watching that always made my stomach feel funny.

I watched as Pop drove off—his smile slowly fading to reveal the look of wistful melancholy that lurked behind even his biggest and warmest smiles. That look had been there for as long as I could remember—long before my mother had headed for the hills, so it wasn't just the result of that. Her leaving didn't help matters, though, and since then I've often had the uneasy feeling I was watching him grow older right before my eyes. Pop wasn't young. He'd been in his mid-forties when he got married, and he turned sixty the year I turned thirteen. As I stood there I could see the way he hunched over the wheel as he rounded the corner and putted toward the elementary school on his way back to Main Street, and I wished there was something I could do to make his life a little easier. And I wished, too, that if he still felt he had to work, he'd at least take on some easier cases—cases where John and Jessie Q. Public didn't take such an active and angry interest. But I knew he wouldn't. Whenever I said anything about it, he'd laugh and tell me, "I've always been a little skittish about being in the majority, Gabriel. The comfort level there is too high for somebody as cantankerous as I am."

Right. The world should be as cantankerous as Pop.

As if worrying about Pop weren't enough, before I even made it to homeroom I'd come to the awful conclusion that I was in love again. With Katie Lyons this time. A freshman. I'd noticed her sweetly shy smile when I passed her in the hall the week before. Then on Friday I happened to fall in behind her on the stairs and noticed that from that angle she was pretty impressive too. Later that day I saw her at her locker and came to the conclusion that her hair was nothing short of spectacular. That's the way it works with me. I start by getting hooked on one part of a girl, and then, often as not, I can feel myself being reeled in by the rest of her. Next thing I know I'm like a fish out of water.

Since seventh grade I've been in and out of love exactly eight times. I try not to let it throw me as much anymore. Long ago I decided that (in addition to the fish-out-of-water thing) falling in love was a little like getting a bad cold—sometimes the symptoms persist longer than others, but it's only a matter of time before you feel like yourself again. Pop told me this was to be expected for somebody my age, an age he referred to as "the white-water section of life's journey." He said that for *his* first twelve or thirteen years he'd been what you might call the model of Irish-Catholic boyhood, following the commandments, serving on the altar, and praying regularly to the Blessed Virgin Mary. But then he'd hit puberty running, as he put it, and that all changed; overnight he turned into a kind of hormonal Mr. Hyde. Naturally, he explained, this knocked a commandment or two for a loop and made it hard for him to look at the Blessed Virgin in quite the same light. He assured me that he eventually adjusted to this new world view and that, knowing me, he had every confidence I'd do the same, and probably in a lot less time than it took him.

I appreciated the thought, but didn't have nearly as much confidence in myself as Pop did in me. While

Pop had charged into puberty, I had the sense that I'd limped into it and, at the rate I was going, would be lucky to make it out at a crawl. Of the eight girls I'd practically lost my mind over, I'd only spoken to three, and of those three I'd only actually asked one out. And by the time I'd worked up the courage to go for it, the major symptoms I'd been experiencing had pretty much run their course and the date had turned out to be kind of anticlimactic. I could only hope this time things would be different.

I saw Katie soon after I'd completed a prehomeroom girl-scouting trip down the freshman hallway. (Girl scouting was a term Pop used to describe the time when, in a beautifully mixed metaphor, his eyes started taking an interest in girls and asked his feet to lend a hand.) At first I thought Katie might be absent. She wasn't at her locker, but her next-door-locker neighbor, Heather Lutz (grandniece of Clutz, I'd heard), was and spotted me on my first pass by. I could feel her watching as I continued down the hall. To make sure this wasn't all in my head, I decided to test it out, acting as if I'd all of a sudden remembered something important and doing a quick U-turn. She was still watching me. And on my way by, I caught her giving the girl next to her what I took to be a there-he-is jab. I groaned inside. This was a complication I didn't need. If *she* liked me, and if she was a friend of Katie's (which she might not be since locker assignments were given out alphabetically), Katie might feel like she had to say no if I ever got around to asking her out. And that was a big *if* in itself.

I was well into this new line of worrying when I almost hit her head-on—Katie, that is. I saw her the last half second before we would have actually collided. She was looking down adjusting her pile of books, and I don't even think she saw me swerve past her. From my particular angle at the time, the thing that struck me was her deep blue eyes. With just that split-second encounter before I veered left, those eyes were already imprinted on my brain. I knew in every fiber of my being that they were the most beautiful eyes I'd ever seen, quiet and enigmatic, as if they contained important secrets of the universe. I hurt—actually felt a wrenching emptiness inside—from just the thought of those eyes.

I stopped and stood for a second to let my head clear. And in that moment I knew without a doubt that Katie Lyons had become my number nine.

I saw Emmett when I was coming out of the gym at the end of fourth period. Instinctively I slammed on my brakes, forcing Bo and a few other guys behind me into a chain-reaction collision. My mind was still kind of reeling from the whole Katie Lyons thing, and I definitely wasn't up for dealing with a human suction cup like Emmett St. Andrews.

Emmett had appeared a month or so earlier, fresh from Salvation House in Albany, and for the last few weeks the whole school had been under a kind of drug siege. Not with real drugs, which had never been a big problem in Wakefield, but with drug *awareness*. Emmett, ex-druggie but still practicing pain in the butt, was relentless. In addition to haranguing us in all our classes and at a Friday evening antidrug rally, he annoyed us more informally throughout the day as a peer pal and some kind of self-proclaimed role model. He'd left for a few weeks and was now back in town preparing for the final phase of his assault—the upcoming field day that was to be the culmination of Wakefield's "Say No to Drugs" campaign.

The way I heard it, Wakefield had applied for and received a fifty-some-thousand-dollar grant to make us aware of drugs. The money was used for: 1. Bringing us Emmett, 2. Buying multiple copies of every antidrug poster ever made, and 3. Sticking up a few DRUG-FREE ZONE signs around school property. As far as I could tell, the only result of this expenditure, except for my being personally offended by having a boob like Emmett brought into my sphere, was a purely unintentional one. Owing to some confusion caused by the proliferation of posters showing fried eggs as "your brain on drugs," one kid in the elementary school supposedly turned his mother in to the police after she cooked his breakfast one morning.

Ironically, right before I spotted Emmett I'd started thinking the morning might be taking a turn for the better. My first three classes had slid by without adding any new worries to my list, and I'd managed to get in five miles on the track during my study hall. Even though track season was over and done with, I still had my permanent pass to go to gym. Running has a way of clearing my head, and I was even thinking that the next time I saw Katie, I might actually talk to her. Only now there was Emmett as large as life and standing there in all his boobocity. I knew from experience that a conversation with him could do a wicked number on my mental state.

Emmett was listening ("active listening" is what he called it) to a couple of junior high kids. The younger kids, and even a lot of the older ones, really thought he was hot stuff because he'd "been there," as he always put it when referring to his drug days, and I figured some of them would end up "being there" themselves so they could be just like him. I hoped the junior high kids didn't have anything major they needed resolved because when Emmett spotted me after the pileup in the gym doorway, he jettisoned his active listening skills (which consisted of rephrasing a speaker's words—nonjudgmentally, of course, and acting like he cared) and started giving the kids the bum's rush.

"I hear ya, man," he said to the earnest-looking kid who'd been doing most of the talking. "I hear ya. Be cool." He held up a hand to be slapped, and that slap was the last and only thing the kid got from a rapidly receding, caring but nonjudgmental Emmett.

"Oh, God," I said to Bo as Emmett approached. "I'm not up for this."

Bo laughed and lifted my arm so that my hand would meet Emmett's hello slap.

"Gabe, my man," Emmett said, parlaying the slap into a hug.

I stood there and got hugged. The only thing on me that moved was my stomach, which I could feel tightening. I knew the reason I was on Emmett's A-list, and it made me want to punch him in the head. It so happened that Emmett had been on the scene with us a few weeks earlier when Pop had caused a commotion on Main Street. Emmett had been staying at Bo's house that whole week because Bo was the head-honcho-captain-commander-in-chief or some such thing of our social worker Bob Chirillo's peer leadership group, which specialized in talking about and putting on skits about drugs and drinking and suicide and other cheerful matters. The fact that Bo was even *in* peer leadership was strange, because in real life he's the last guy who would sit around discussing any of these things. But Bo's pretty much into every school activity there is—sports, band, politics (he's class president), student council, you name it—and that's the kind of person peer leadership recruits.

Anyway, that whole week Emmett had been at the school talking to us—no, Emmett's word was *educating* us—not only about the dangers of drugs and alcohol, but also about things like model cement and Wite-Out used "inappropriately," and that Friday evening was the big drug awareness rally in the school auditorium. And because Emmett was the type who really got off telling everybody how far down he'd been, and how his family was dysfunctional, and how many different drugs he'd taken in his life and in what combinations, and how many times he'd woken up in alleyways in neighborhoods that were tougher and meaner than anything we'd ever seen living in a nothing-happening place like Wakefield, and because Bob Chirillo and Ray Phineas, our Barney Fife D.A.R.E. officer, were both in seventh heaven basking in Emmett's reflected glory and whenever they could adding their own two cents worth, which generally grew into folding money, the panel discussion ran way overtime. So I didn't get to check on Pop as early as I should have, and he overdid it at Willie's. Charlie did manage to get Pop's keys so he wouldn't drive, but Pop, after a while, had set off for further adventures on foot.

And it just so happened that right after the rally let out, Pop was coming out of the Cloud Nine tavern and, by this time, was feeling no pain. Our village's traffic light—the only one we had unless you counted the one out by the Kmart plaza, which was technically outside the village limits—had already switched to its blinking mode for the night, and traffic was starting to back up behind the flashing red. Pop, who tended to be public-spirited with or without the inspiration of alcohol, must have thought he could be of some assistance here and waded out into the intersection and began waving his arms in the hope of getting things moving. The actual effect of this was to clog things up even more, and by the time we reached the intersection in Emmett's Grand Am (with the personalized SAY NO plates), traffic was backed up toward the school as far as you could see. I ignored (but didn't forget) Emmett's head-shaking and sigh of disgust as we all saw what was going on at the intersection. Bo and I jumped out of the car, grabbed Pop, and although Emmett wasn't exactly thrilled by the transaction, poured him into the backseat. We barely made it out of there before we saw the flashing lights of the Chief's car trying to squeeze past the stalled traffic. Later, after we got Pop safely home and had come back into town for his car, I felt a hand on my shoulder as I started to get out of Emmett's passenger seat. The hand was attached to Emmett. His face was twisted into the caring attitude that people like him get, and I knew he was up for some active listening. "You want to talk about it, my friend?" he said.

And the sad thing was, from then on I *was* his friend. Because Pop got drunk and waved his arms around a little on Main Street, until the next evening when he returned to Albany, Emmett was stuck to me like gum on a shoe. *Concerned* gum.

"Gabe, and my main man, Bo," he said. He slapped Bo's hand and then wrapped us both in a football huddle hug before I could step wide. "How goes it with my posse?" he said after he let us go.

"Jim-dandy," Bo said. "Yourself?"

"Taking things one day at a time," Emmett said

instructively. "One day at a time." He aimed his caring face at me. "And how're you doing, G-man? Hanging in there?"

"It's Gabe," I said.

"You'll make it, man," he said, his voice dripping with reassurance. "You're like me. You're a survivor."

Before I could collect myself enough to frame a suitable response to that, Emmett clapped a hand on Bo's shoulder and said, "Got a minute, Bo-man? We need to finalize some plans for Saturday."

Bo shrugged. "Well, I have English. . . ."

Emmett gave him a drugs-take-precedence-over-that shake of the head. "Bob'll cover you there. We gotta keep getting the message out, and to do it right we need to get busy. We wanna make sure this is the biggest thing that ever happened to this one-horse town."

"Yeah, right," I said, thinking that if we did only have one horse, I knew where to find its behind. I didn't get to share this thought, though, because Emmett was already striding down the hall with Bo. As I watched them leave I was suddenly aware of a strange feeling. Lurking beneath my relief at having gotten free of Emmett so quickly was a vague but unpleasant sense that I'd been dumped as unceremoniously as the two junior high kids. For that day, at least, Emmett felt he had bigger fish to fry.

Emmett was gone before lunch, which was fine with me. He and his SAY NO license plates had to roll off to another school where he'd "get busy" and serve up his drug message to another captive audience. If he was lucky, they'd have more kids there who actually did drugs. And if we were lucky, they'd keep him.

In the cafeteria Sudie told us she'd finished patching

up Rosasharn's burnt swamp thing costume and was coming along on the other two costumes she was making—one for Jeremy, and one for Ethan. Jeremy didn't know it yet, but Bo and I had decided that the unique chemistry that existed between Rosasharn and him made him the perfect choice to play Green Guy's wife, Green Gal, complete with green wig, a set of oversized lips, and a couple of decent-sized breasts, courtesy of a padded bra. Ethan, making his film debut, would round out the family as their son Greenie. As long as it wasn't a speaking part, Ethan was glad to do it, but we knew we'd have to handle Jeremy a little more carefully. We figured if we told him about it right away, that'd leave him enough time to rant and rave and swear up and down that he wasn't getting into any stupid costume and making a fool of himself, especially if it meant being married to "that stupid tub," and by Friday night his resistance would be low and we'd have him.

When I saw Jeremy heading our way along with Rosasharn, I poked Bo. Sudie knew what was up and smiled.

"Ah," Rosasharn said, plunking his tray down next to Sudie's, "the love of my life and my dear friends."

"I wish you wouldn't call me the love of your life," I said. "People will talk."

"He didn't mean *you*," Jeremy said, all indignant, as he slid onto the bench next to Rosasharn.

I mouthed the words "It's too easy" to Bo and he smiled. Rosasharn leaned across the table and tried to kiss me.

"You wanna take that for me, Jeremy?" I said. "You're closer."

Jeremy picked up his fork, all set to fend off Rosasharn's lips, which had already switched directions and were heading his way. "Don't, ya stupid tub," he said, "unless you want a fork stuck in your head."

Rosasharn gave him the Curly wave-off.

"Unrequited love makes me sad," I said, and then realized I was only half joking.

"You oughta know," Jeremy told me, and was so surprised by this burst of wit that his face almost broke into a smile.

"Speaking of affairs of the heart," Bo said, spotting the perfect segue, "Friday night we start filming the scenes with Green Guy's loving, dedicated, and stunningly green wife."

"Who'd marry that tub?" Jeremy said from behind his hamburger.

"Love's a funny thing," I said. "Sometimes it's the ones you least expect who end up getting together."

"You know, I've noticed that," Bo said. "Did you ever notice that, Jeremy?"

At first Jeremy looked disgusted that we'd waste our breath talking about something so stupid, but then all of a sudden he stopped chewing and got a funny look on his face. When he looked over at us, we smiled at him and nodded.

"Uh-uh," he said, his whole body squaring off in opposition to the idea. "Uh-uh. Forget it. I ain't doin' it." He went back to eating and tried to act as if he'd given the final word on the subject. Only every few minutes he'd have to look our way and announce it all over again. "I ain't doin' it. No way."

We kept smiling and nodding our heads at him. Jeremy didn't know it yet, of course, but he was already as good as in that green wig and falsies.

Seven

Chow time at Blood Red Pond was a fairly predictable affair. Rosasharn and Jeremy would get a rip-roaring fire going and then proceed to cook up and finish off an almost lethal number of hot dogs and hamburgers, and then top those off with a ton or two of s'mores, which in case you don't know, are marshmallows and chocolate melted between graham crackers over an open fire. Sudie, in what she believed to be a sensible regard for balanced nutrition, would insist they eat at least some of her macaroni or potato salad, depending on what she had made earlier that day, either of which contained enough mayo to constrict whatever small openings may have been left in their poor crud-clogged arteries. Bo was the flip side—always bringing all kinds of fresh fruit and maybe a green salad with slivered almonds or something like a fresh avocado salad, which Jeremy would always examine with exaggerated disgust, demanding to know why he didn't eat *real* food.

Ethan and I probably had it the best, being able to pick and choose from both culinary extremes as well as having plenty of our own favorites (what Jeremy called "yuppie chow")—things like pesto pasta, Cajun shrimp, tabouli, and different ethnic foods that Pop would pick up for the weekend from Glens Falls or Saratoga or Albany, wherever business happened to take him at the end of the week. Also, Pop prided himself on having a fairly discriminating sweet tooth, and over the years he'd scouted out the area for the best of the best. That night we had éclairs and some chocolate raspberry layer cake from The Vanilla Bean in South Troy. Except for the desserts, most of what we brought rubbed Jeremy the wrong way, the same as Bo's stuff did, and this particular Friday night was no different.

"What this?" he demanded, pulling the top off one of the containers Pop had picked up from our favorite Indian restaurant.

"Malai kofte," I told him, and braced myself for the assault. One of Jeremy's specialties was matching up different foods to disgusting things they looked like. I'd become fairly resistant to this over the years, but occasionally he'd still get me by coming up with something sickening even by his standards.

This time Jeremy decided to spread his message of good cheer around a little before zeroing in on me. His eyes flicked over to Ethan, who was sitting beside me looking through an old Superman comic. "You think Tarzan eats this crap?" he said, waving the Malai kofte at him.

Ethan shrugged. "I don't know. It's Superman I like."

"I can just hear it," Jeremy continued. "'Uh, excuse me, Jane, but could you pass the *Malai kofte,* please?'" he said in this mincing voice.

"It's Indian," Ethan explained reasonably. "And Tarzan wasn't in India."

"Neither are you, but *you* eat it." Jeremy waited to see if Ethan had an answer for that before turning his attention back to the Malai kofte and then to me. "You know what this looks like?" he said, and scowled some more into the container.

"No," I said. "But I bet you'll tell me."

"Look at it," he demanded. "It looks like calf scours. What'd you do—hold this up behind some calf that had the runs?" He made a farty kind of noise and held the container out for a mock fill-up.

I rolled my eyes and grabbed the thing from him. "Did you get dropped on your head as a baby?"

"No."

"Too bad. It might've done you some good."

"At least I don't eat calf scours."

"Calf scours?" Rosasharn said, looking up from the other side of a rack of hamburgers he'd rigged up over the fire. "And why wasn't I told you were bringing something so scrumptileeicious?"

Without meaning to, I found myself looking at the Malai kofte in my hands. It had always been one of my favorite things, but now, thanks to Jeremy, I was seeing it in a whole new light. It was lumpy and brownish yellow and *did* look a little like calf scours, now that he pointed it out.

Meanwhile Jeremy had whipped the cover off the Navratan korma, which is mixed vegetables and Indian cheese in a cream sauce. His nose was giving it a good going-over, and then he made like he was throwing up into it. "Look," he said, holding it out. "Chunks."

That did it. I almost gagged. It wasn't just Jeremy's skill as a gross-out artist that got me. My appetite had been taking a nosedive all week, like it always does when I fall head over heels for a girl. That pining-away feeling I had for Katie had continued to grow each day until I was well on the road to being a basket case. Looking back on it, my whole week had been like something out of *The Twilight Zone*. In addition to the mental agony, a fair amount of roughness had been seeping onto my physical plane as well. For starters, I was losing stuff left and right. My Adidas turned up missing on Wednesday, a rugby shirt on Thursday, and some money

I had lying around just that morning. Not only that, but strange things were happening in our refrigerator too. Stuff that I was the only one in the whole house who ate was disappearing from one day to the next, and I didn't remember eating it. I didn't even remember having a decent enough appetite to *want* to eat it. I've always been absentminded but this was getting out of hand. My mind was out taking a walk around the block.

"Eat it if you think it's so good," Jeremy ordered, thrusting the Navratan korma he'd been entertaining himself with farther under my chin and studying me with his gestapo face.

"Or perhaps you'd like to wrap yon face around yon former cow," Rosasharn said, coming at me with the sizzling burger rack, "and save yon barf and calf scours for dessert."

I tried not to but must have looked a little green as the burger fumes hit my nostrils. "Maybe later," I said as casually as I could manage.

"All right," Jeremy said. "Who is it this time?" He'd finally sat down and was scowling at me from across the fire.

I scowled back at him. "What are you *talking* about?"

"Cut the crap. Whenever you sit around looking pitiful like that and won't eat, it always means you've gone stupid over some girl again."

I couldn't believe he'd nailed it like that. I looked around. Everybody else was studying me now, even Ethan, whose face had come up out of his comic book. Bo shrugged. I'd already told him about Katie Lyons, and it's always that much harder to lie if even one person knows you're lying. Especially if that person is an honest one.

I closed my eyes and took a deep breath. "All right," I said after a while. "But this doesn't go any farther than here. You understand?" I gave Jeremy the eye, and then Rosasharn.

Rosasharn went through the motions of zipping his lips and throwing away the key. Jeremy didn't feel it necessary to make any deals. "Just tell us, Gabe-boy." He deliberately ran the two words together so it sounded like "Gay boy."

I took a breath. "It's Katie Lyons. She's a freshman."

"Katie Lyons!" Sudie practically screamed. "I know her! She's been best friends with Heather Lutz ever since they were in first grade. Heather lives right down the street from me. I see her walking past my house every day!"

"Oh, boy," Jeremy said. "She walks past your house."

My heart sank to a record low. Heather was the one I'd seen giving me the once-over earlier in the week.

"I can put in a good word for you," Sudie said. "I've known Heather for forever."

I shook my head. That was the last thing I needed. "Thanks, but I'll handle it."

"Issa so beautiful," Rosasharn said, pretending to burst into tears. "Thissa young love issa so beautiful, I'ma tellin' you." He pulled out a handkerchief and honked into it.

"He's not gonna ask her out," Jeremy said.

"I'll do it," I told him, hoping to convince myself at the same time I was convincing him. "I don't see *you* asking that many girls out."

"I do whenever I want to," he said. "I just don't give

up eating and get all spastic like you do."

"Issa *so* beautiful," Rosasharn said, bursting into a fresh round of sobs.

"I said I'd ask her out and I will," I told Jeremy over the racket Rosasharn was making. "So don't worry about it."

"When?" he demanded in that stubborn way of his.

I shrugged. "There's not much going on at the school this time of year. Maybe in a couple of weeks I'll ask her to a movie or something."

"What's wrong with that drug thing?"

"What drug thing?"

"That stupid drug thing they're having tomorrow. Ask her to that."

I looked around. Everybody was still studying me pretty good. Bo was wearing the little half smile he usually gets whenever I'm in the middle of one of those exchanges with Jeremy. Ethan looked a little stricken— like he wanted to help but couldn't think of a way to do it.

I turned back to Jeremy and shook my head. "Too short notice," I said. "Besides, a drug field day isn't exactly a date kind of thing."

"Buk, buk, buk." Jeremy flapped his arms like chicken wings.

"Why don't *you* ask somebody, mouth?"

"You mean a real live *girl?*" he said in mock horror. "Oh, I'm so *scared.*" He went back to his Jeremy voice. "I will if you will." And then back to his chicken voice. "Buk, buk, buk."

You'd think at my age I'd be mature enough not to be goaded into decisions by a sour-faced guy making chicken noises. And you'd be wrong.

"No sweat," I said, hoping my voice held steady.

"We'll do it tomorrow morning." Just saying it gave me a little burst of courage. I grabbed the container of Malai kofte, stuck a fork in it, and took a big bite. "This stuff's good," I said. "You oughta try it."

"Hey, scrub."

I lowered my Emerson book and looked up to see Jeremy scowling at me from the other side of the campfire. He sat there gawking away but didn't say anything more. "*What?*" I said finally.

"You got your stupid face in that book, and you don't even know when people are talking to you," he said.

"So talk," I told him, and closed the book. It was strange, but after agreeing to ask Katie out, I'd started feeling more like myself than I had all week.

"I wasn't the one talking to you," Jeremy said. "Why would I wanna talk to you?"

Ethan tapped me on the knee and pointed at Sudie, who being used to this kind of cross fire, was waiting patiently. "I asked what you were reading," she told me.

"Oh," I said. "Sorry. It's something Pop got me—a collection of Emerson's essays and poems."

"You mean the Emerson we did in *school*?" You could tell she wasn't a big fan.

I nodded. "It's kind of fascinating actually." I flipped the book back open and tried to find the right page. "Listen to this. . . ."

"Oh, God," Jeremy moaned. "He's gonna read to us."

I found the paragraph I'd been looking for and twisted around so some light from the fire would shine on the page. "Listen," I said, and started in.

> *If malice and vanity wear the coat of phil-*
> *anthropy, shall that pass? If an angry bigot*
> *assumes this bountiful cause of abolition,*
> *and comes to me with his last news from*
> *Barbados, why should I not say to him, "Go*
> *love thy infant; love thy woodchopper; be*
> *good-natured and modest; have that grace;*
> *and never varnish your hard uncharitable*
> *ambition with this incredible tenderness for*
> *black folk a thousand miles away. Thy love*
> *afar is spite at home."*

I looked up at everybody. Bo was wearing the same smile he'd had during my discussion with Jeremy earlier. Ethan was studying me with big serious eyes the way he often does. Jeremy was scowling. Sudie had kind of a politely blank look.

Rosasharn broke the ice. "Attsa so beautiful," he said, and started sobbing harder even than he had earlier.

"Does anybody see any black folk around here?" Jeremy wanted to know.

"No, no, that's not the point," I said, getting all excited. "Don't you get it? He's talking about people like Emmett St. Andrews."

"Oh, God," Jeremy said. "Here we go again. And which guy was Emmett supposed to be, scrubby—the woodcutter or the infant?"

I glanced at Bo. He folded his arms and his smile got a little bigger.

"Neither," I said, being too used to Jeremy to let myself get pulled too far off-line. "He's the *bigot*. Don't you get it? Emerson was talking about people like Emmett—people who run around acting like these great do-gooders, but they're really not even nice people. See, Emmett spends all his time traveling around the countryside pretending to care about people like us he doesn't even know. And meanwhile he's treating all the *real* people in his life, the people he really knows, like crap. He tells anybody who'll listen all about how his family is dysfunctional, and describes in detail every time they didn't praise him enough, or every time somebody looked at him the wrong way and damaged his self-esteem. . . . I'm telling you," I said, thumping on the book, "this is Emmett to a T. It's Bob Chirillo and all of them."

Jeremy snorted. "Every time he reads a book or sees a movie, he thinks it's about Bob Chirillo or . . ." He snapped his fingers. "Who's that lady he always used to go off on? What was her name?"

"Mrs. Quinby," Bo said, looking at me and shrugging as if he'd been subpoenaed and had no choice but to answer.

"He's like *obsessed* with those people," Jeremy said, getting into the mood of the whole thing and waving his arms around.

"Obsessed" may have been a little strong, but there was no denying that everyone there had had to sit through at least a few of my tirades about Mrs. Quinby and Bob Chirillo. Mrs. Quinby, the elementary and middle school psychologist, was kind of like a firefighter who liked fires a little too much. Only her fires consisted of people's problems. Within two days after my mother took off with the embezzler, Mrs. Quinby had me in her office for a chat, trying to fan the embers of any damage my mother's departure may have done to my psyche. Even though (or maybe *because*) I told her I was fine, she decided I must be crying out for help. Before I knew it she had me officially enrolled in WAFA (standing for "We Are Families Also"), an after-school thing for kids from broken homes. In WAFA what we did most of the time was sat in a circle and told each other about (or drew pictures about) how sad we were and how difficult everything was and clapped for anybody who told a really pitiful story, and clapped and *cheered* if they broke down and cried. But this was a barrel of laughs compared to the recreation part of the meetings. We used to play a hide-and-seek kind of game, only we weren't looking for each other—we were looking for little scraps of paper with brilliant messages on them like "I am special" and "I like myself just the way I am," or the fun-filled and informative, "My parents' divorce was not my fault." And when you found one of these scraps (which wasn't hard since they weren't even really hidden), you had to read it out to the group and they'd all clap for you and Mrs. Quinby would act thrilled that everyone was having such a good time and achieving sound mental health to boot.

I quit WAFA one afternoon after throwing what normal people might call a tantrum (Mrs. Quinby called it a breakthrough). I'd had a bad day at school, and Mrs. Quinby, as soon as she saw I was in a lousy mood, started moving in on me with her hook and ladder. She'd made it her personal goal to get me to share my feelings for the benefit of her and the other kids. Mostly her. At first I wouldn't say anything, but she didn't let up, so finally I let her have it. I told her we should play games that were fun for a change instead of stupid things with messages that weren't even hard to find. Mrs. Quinby did a fair job of keeping her smile intact and told me *she* felt that the games we played *were* fun and, possibly, was there something else troubling me—something deeper? I didn't answer, so, no doubt to prime my emotional pump, she announced it might be a good time to play "The Feelings Game." This was kind of a board ("bored" would be more accurate) game where each square contained the name of a feeling such as "jealous" or "hurt" or "happy," and whatever one you landed on, you had to tell the group about a time you felt that way. When Mrs. Quinby, her whole face wreathed in that infuriating smile of hers, handed me the dice and suggested that maybe I'd like to go first, I took them and heaved them out the window, at the same time saying what I hoped was a very un-WAFA-like thing concerning her family tree. When I told Pop what I'd done, he had me go to her office the next day to apologize, but he also agreed that I didn't have to go to any more WAFA meetings.

It was a major setback for Mrs. Quinby, but she didn't give up without a fight. Until the day I got out of middle school I had the sense she was keeping me under close surveillance, and twice she suited up and came after me—once right after Margaret died, to try to teach me to grieve by numbers, and another time right after Pop had gone on a particularly colorful binge, to try to get me to join some kind of children of alcoholics group. Both times I came close to having another "breakthrough" in her office, but I held back, knowing that Pop would ask me to apologize to her, and I never wanted to put myself in that position again. When I entered junior high, Bob Chirillo decided he needed to get *his* therapeutic paws on me, and then finally Emmett. The whole bunch of them made me sick.

"Uh, excuse me," Jeremy was saying in a voice that was supposed to be mine, "but I just saw *The Wizard of*

Oz and I think the Tin Man is supposed to stand for Bob Chirillo."

"You're very amusing," I told him. "Or is it just your face that makes you seem funny?"

"Uh, excuse me," Jeremy continued, "but I just saw *Jaws,* and I think the shark was supposed to be Mrs. . . . uh, what's-her-face?" He snapped his fingers.

"Quinby," Bo said, and then gave me that same subpoenaed shrug again.

"Yeah," Jeremy said in his own voice, and then continued on as me. "Uh, excuse me, but I just saw *Lassie Come Home,* and I think Lassie is . . ."

By now we were all cracked up—even Ethan, who'd put his comic book aside for the performance. "Lassie's a *dog.*" Ethan said, giggling.

"Yeah," Jeremy said as himself before going on with the routine. "I think Lassie's supposed to be Ray Phineas, the D.A.R.E. guy."

"Wrong," I said, laughing. "Lassie has a higher IQ."

Rosasharn piped in with a bad Irish accent. "Oh, and 'tis always a good weekend that begins with Gabriel O'Roiley up on his high horse, doncha know."

"All right, all right," I said. "You guys can make fun, but you have to admit there's something wrong with that crowd. Searching around for any little problem they can talk to death."

"Yeah, just what you're doin'," Jeremy said.

"Shut up," I told him. Then I looked at Bo. His smile had widened and was taking on some definite characteristics of a smirk.

"You're just a bundle of support tonight, aren't you, buddy?" I said, tapping him lightly on the head.

Bo laughed and tapped me back. "We'd miss it if you stopped doing this," he said.

"I wouldn't," Jeremy said, and threw another log on the fire. Then he picked up a stick and pointed it at Ethan. "Anything you'd like to share from Tarzan?" he asked him.

Ethan shook his head. Unlike me, he knew when to keep his mouth shut.

• • •

Sudie did a good job on the costumes. Jeremy's wasn't half bad—well worth the trouble of getting him into it, especially since most of that hassle took place while Rosasharn and I went into town for Pop. By the time I'd driven Pop home and walked back to Blood Red Pond, Jeremy was all decked out as Green Gal. In the light of the campfire, not only did he look a little like a real swamp creature, but with his red lips and green breasts I could see how something that just crawled out of the swamp might even find him attractive. Rosasharn seemed to agree. After he transformed himself into Green Guy and saw Jeremy as Green Gal, he let out what was supposed to be, I guess, some kind of swamp mating call and took off after him. On their second pass by the fire, Sudie snagged him. "You're gonna ruin the costumes," she said, and poked him in the head.

Ethan looked good too—just as shy and quiet in his costume as out of it. When I first saw him I had to laugh—a little green swamp thing sitting in front of the fire reading Superman.

We managed to get some pretty good footage, I thought, of family life in the swamp with Green Guy, the bad-tempered father, and Green Gal, the cringing wife (except when Rosasharn stepped out of character to be affectionate and Jeremy stepped out of character to belt him), and Greenie, their brilliant but at least slightly maladjusted son who sat around with a book called *Cognitive Strategies for Qualitative Enhancement of Reading Comprehension* which Bo's mom had lent us. She used it in Advanced Placement English as an example of how supposedly intelligent people can do a number on the language.

A couple of times I caught Ethan looking off into the woods as if he'd spotted something, but when I asked him what he saw, he just gave me a little shrug. Ethan has this way of seeing things before he actually *sees* them almost, so I didn't bother looking too hard where he was looking. I have trouble spotting things even when Ethan is patiently pointing them out to me, so I didn't expect to be able to see something he wasn't even sure of. Plus I was kept pretty busy helping with setups for shots, not to mention refereeing the skirmishes between Jeremy and Rosasharn. I also had to deal with Jeremy one on one. It became his personal goal to see that I didn't forget for one minute my agreement to ask Katie Lyons to the drug field day. Like clockwork between shots he'd amble over to taunt me with his off-key, sour-faced rendition of Little Orphan Annie singing like a broken record, "Tomorrow, tomorrow . . . Tomorrow, tomorrow."

"No sweat," I'd say every time he got done singing in my face. "No sweat."

Eight

The last bale dropped off the side of the conveyor. I heaved it over to Jeremy, who was stacking along the roofline a little below me. A few seconds later both the elevator and conveyor stopped, ending the nerve-wracking screech the chains made as they slid along the metal trays. I collapsed onto the bale behind me. It had to be at least one hundred and ten degrees in that haymow. Jeremy's father had never made the switch to haylage, which was the way more and more farmers brought in their early hay—chopped and blown into an automatic unloading wagon and then shot through a blower into a silo without ever being touched by a human hand. And he didn't go for those giant round bales that you left sitting around outside until you needed them either. So there we were in that sauna of a haymow doing grunt work.

"You look like a wet rat," Jeremy said, coming over to where I was and sitting on the side of the conveyor.

"And *you* don't?" I said, looking up at him. We'd long since pulled our shirts off and were both slimy with sweat. I grabbed my shirt off a beam and wiped the sweat out of my eyes.

"Anybody alive up there?" we heard through the opening in the side of the barn where the elevator attached to the conveyor. It was Jeremy's father, calling from the hay wagon below.

"No," Jeremy yelled down.

"Sorry I don't have any more to send you boys just now, but that's it for a few minutes." You could hear the laughter in his voice. He'd spent enough time in sweltering haymows in his day to know what we were going through.

"Ha, ha," Jeremy said, not even having the energy to make his voice carry to down below.

"Don't you worry though," his father continued. "I'll be back quick as I can with a fresh load." His laughter wafted up through the haymow doorway.

At one time I actually started thinking Jeremy must have been adopted. His parents were two of the most jovial people you'd ever want to meet, and they both seemed to enjoy nothing more than a good laugh. Even their property was set up for laughs. In addition to a second mailbox perched about ten feet over their regular box and labeled "air mail," they also had the full line of yuk-yuk lawn ornaments, including the bending-over fat lady and the little boy who's dropped his drawers and is supposedly peeing in the bushes. This adoption theory was making more and more sense to me until one day when I happened to be sitting on the Wulfsons' porch waiting for Jeremy to come in from the field. I hadn't waited very long before I spotted him walking across his yard toward me. Not knowing anybody was there watching, he stopped and did a second take at the fat lady's backside (that's the only side she had, really), and all of a sudden he actually began to smile—a real, regular-person kind of smile. He wiped it off his face as soon as he saw me, of course, but by then I already knew: Jeremy was a closet humorist.

"Well, get going, rat boy," Jeremy said, looking down at me from the conveyor.

"Get going where?" I asked.

"Weren't you gonna call your little *sweetie?*" he said, puckering up his face on the word "sweetie." "Or have you chickened out already?"

I had actually forgotten, which goes to show just how hot that haymow was. "You were gonna call *your* sweetie too," I reminded him.

"I know," Jeremy said, and then started doing this spastic shaking on the conveyor. "Oh, I'm *so* scared."

"Don't worry," I said, acting as cool as I could manage under the circumstances. "I doubt any female would say yes to you anyway. Not one of the higher primates, at least."

We climbed down through the nearest chute and headed for the milk house. Jeremy reached for the hose used to wash the milk tank and turned on the faucet. After drinking from the end of the hose, he started rinsing off his arms, which is a good way to begin cooling down after a tough session in a haymow. I started doing the same thing at the faucet to one of the large stainless-steel sinks. When I turned around again, Jeremy was bent over (like the fat lady on his lawn) spraying water over his face and through his hair.

"You're getting good at that, Jeremy," I told him. "One of these days I bet your parents'll start letting you use the shower in the house."

"Shut up, ribsy," he said, and shot some cold water my way.

The ribsy thing was an exaggeration. Jeremy was every bit as lean as I was, although he was probably a little more muscular—I'll give him that. He had what I always thought of as one of the basic farm boy builds. There's pudgy farm boy and there's wiry farm boy, and Jeremy was definitely the latter.

"Well?" I said, taking a deep breath. "Are we gonna do it?"

"What's the big deal? You just do it." He grabbed the phone book, found the number he wanted, snatched up the receiver to the wall phone near the doorway, and started dialing. I have to admit—I was impressed.

"Hello, Amy?" he said, after what must've been only about two rings. "This is Jeremy Wulfson. You wanna go to that drug thing with me this afternoon?" As he paused for the answer, the look on his face changed, first to a look of puzzlement and then back to its usual deadpan. "Oh," he said after a while. "Okay. Yeah. Bye"

"Well?" I said when he hung up. "What'd she say?"

"Nuthin'," he told me.

"Whaddaya mean nothing? You asked her out, and then you stood there listening. She musta said *something*."

"It was her mother."

"Her *mother*?" I started laughing. "Didn't you make sure you had Amy before you started asking her out?"

He shrugged. "I thought I did, but her mother's name must be Amy too."

This whole thing was cracking me up more by the minute. And the thing I found the funniest about it was that Jeremy really didn't see any humor in the situation at all. *Nada*. And not because he was embarrassed or disappointed or anything like that. He just plain didn't think it was funny. To him it just didn't stack up to the plywood fat lady bending over in his yard or the bare-butted kid peeing in his bushes. The more I thought about it, the more I cracked up, until I was practically lying across the milk tank and howling.

"How was I supposed to know?" he said. "I've never heard of a girl being named after her mother."

I hadn't either, but that didn't make it any less funny to me. "So what'd she say?" I asked when I could speak again. "What'd Amy *senior* say?"

"She told me the other Amy was at church camp for

the weekend, and she didn't figure I'd want to take *her*, which she was right about because I've seen her, and I said 'okay' and hung up."

"Oh, God," I said, straightening up and wiping my eyes. "Why couldn't I have had Bo's video camera? The rest of humanity shouldn't be deprived of this."

"Shut up and make *your* call, Gabe-boy," he said, and stuck the phone in my face.

Seeing the phone close-up like that had a sobering effect on me. Jeremy noticed the difference and pressed his advantage. "Take it in your *hand*," he said in a Mr. Rogers voice. "Now put it up to your *ear*. And then you *dial*."

"If you were really Mr. Rogers, you wouldn't tell me what to do," I said. "You'd ask me how I feel about it."

"Shut up," Jeremy said, reverting to his regular personality. "Just dial the stupid phone."

"You're so touchy," I told him, and started dialing. You'll notice I didn't need any phone book. Katie's number had already been imprinted on my brain after one glance at it, the same as her eyes had been earlier in the week.

I was pretty nervous when I was dialing, but the full force of what I was doing didn't actually hit me until I heard the first ring. Then my heart started racing like mad. For a few seconds I wasn't sure if I'd even be able to speak.

Somebody picked up the phone and said hello. It was a female voice but I knew it wasn't Katie. I'd heard little snippets of her conversations during some of my girl-scouting trips down the freshman hallway, and there was no way I'd mistake her voice. I even heard it in my dreams.

"May I speak to Katie?" I was finally able to blurt out.

"I'm sorry," the voice said. "She's with her father right now. Could I take a message?"

I kind of froze for a second—not sure if I should leave my name or not.

"Ah, no . . . I'll . . . I'll call again sometime. Thanks."

I took the phone down from my ear and stood there with it. I was still wrestling with the notion of whether I should have left my name or a message. If I'd done that at least I wouldn't have to start from scratch the next time I called. Which would be *when?* I hadn't even asked if she was gone for the morning, for the day, or for the whole weekend.

Jeremy yanked the receiver out of my hand and hung it up. "We put the phone back when we're through," he said in his Mr. Rogers voice. "So much to learn and such a dumb student."

I leaned back against the wall and took a couple of deep breaths. I could feel Jeremy's eyes on me, so I took another one—an extra long one—just to make him wait.

"*Well,* Scrubby?" he said before I'd even finished inhaling.

"No luck," I said. "She wasn't home."

Jeremy scowled about that for a minute. "Maybe she knew it was you calling," he offered finally.

I walked over and leaned on the tank alongside him. "Look," I said, "Just because I struck out, that's no reason you should have to go to the drug day alone."

"Whaddaya mean?"

I looked him in the eye. "Here's what I'm thinking: Why don't you get over there, pick up that phone, and call Amy's mom back before somebody else asks her."

I was quick enough to avoid the headlock, but he caught me with a wicked thump to my back as he chased me out the door.

Nine

I have one of those minds that kicks into overdrive at the drop of a hat, and whenever it does the world around me tends to fade into kind of a background noise. This can sometimes cause difficulties for those in my general vicinity—in this case Jeremy, who was back to stacking hay a little below me. A few different times I landed bales on top of him, which didn't do anything to improve his disposition. After he got whaled the third time, he decided that *he* should be the one working up by the conveyor.

The thing was, I couldn't get my mind off Katie Lyons and the call I'd just made. Part of me was still giving myself grief for not leaving a message, and part of me was still glad I didn't. Part of me was disappointed that Katie wouldn't be going to the drug rally with me, and part of me was actually *relieved* about the whole thing, if you can figure that out. After my mind had slalomed through those issues for a while, it slid into the whole notion of Katie herself. Ever since I'd discovered her I'd had this image of her as coming from one of those *Leave it to Beaver* kinds of families you know with two parents waiting at home whose lives pretty much revolved around her. (For some reason I'd assumed she was an only child although I didn't know that for a fact.) Now I was coming up with a whole different picture. Her mother (the lady I *think* was her mother) had said she was with her father, which at the time I'd taken to mean that she'd *gone* someplace with him. But as I pored over those few words again and again in that sweltering haymow I started thinking that what her mother had meant was that she was *with* her father—like for the whole weekend. Which meant (I was becoming more sure of it by the minute) that her parents must be divorced or separated.

This sudden realization gave me a funny feeling in the pit of my stomach. All I could think about was how she must spend her time being yanked back and forth between her two parents, loving them both and feeling guilty and miserable about one whenever she was with the other. Meanwhile they were both trying desperately to come up with ways to win her over to their side (even in this new version I still had her down as the center of their existence). The more I played this over in my mind, the more dramatic and tragic it seemed, and the bigger and hollower the feeling in the pit of my stomach grew until I found myself pleading with her to believe it wasn't her fault, that *she* was an innocent victim in all of this. I was so caught up in the whole thing that it didn't dawn on me at the time that this was pretty much the same kind of spiel Mrs. Quinby fired off with mind-numbing regularity at her WAFA meetings. All I knew was that *I* wanted to be the one to save Katie from the excruciating torment she must be experiencing as a result of this parental tug-of-war. Over and over in my mind's eye I set her parents straight once and for all. After dealing with that, I saw myself taking Katie to the movies and on long walks (or on drives when I got my license) and giving her the kind of pressure-free existence to which she was entitled. Her parents would resent me at first, maybe, seeing only how I was stealing their precious daughter's heart, but then they'd come around and see that I was right, that their behavior had been out of line, and that I was giving her a new life, a life of happiness and fulfillment she'd never known before.

At this point a bale slammed into my back and I came close to ripping my scalp open on a few of the roofing nails poking down a few inches from my head. I pulled the bale off me and gave Jeremy dirty look.

"Oh, *I'm* sorry," he said in a mincing voice. "I must have been *daydreaming*. I'm just awful like that." Then he fired another bale at me which I managed to snag in time and shove up under the eaves. This didn't put a complete stop to my Katie speculations or my different savior scenarios, but it did pull the here-and-now world of the haymow into at least a partial focus, and it was harder for Jeremy to catch me off guard during the rest of the load.

When I got home and hit the shower, my mind, knowing it was out of physical danger there, was off and running again, tearing into Katie's parents with a vengeance. In one version I even had to block a swing from her father and hold him down while I set him straight. Later, as I helped Ethan tow Cappy around the yard, I was still rewriting and editing the whole scene. Ethan must have known something was up, but he's pretty used to me drifting off like that and he didn't say anything.

Rosasharn and Jeremy came by at about two. Sudie was at the school already, being one of the volunteers who'd be organizing the kids' games and then helping serve the barbecue in the evening. Ditto for Bo, who'd also be on stage afterward to introduce speakers and what not.

We dropped Ethan off at Pop's office, and he gave me his little wave as we pulled away. Then we drove over and helped Rosasharn sweep out the laundromat and collect the change and fix a washing machine that had been acting up. Finally we headed for the school.

Half the town was already there, it seemed, and we spent some time wandering around the athletic field watching different kids' games and races, which were just getting under way. I kind of wished I'd talked Ethan into signing up for a few of the races at least, but then again he always looked forward to helping Pop on Saturdays, so maybe it was just as well I hadn't. I kept my eyes peeled for Katie but didn't see her. Before too long Sudie spotted us and put us to work helping set up tables on the football field. The chickens were already barbecuing and volunteers were going up and down the rows of makeshift steel barbecue pits basting and turning them. Emmett was there, striding importantly from the games to the barbecue to the tables, delivering instructions (and an occasional manly hug) and holding small summit meetings with Bob Chirillo and Ray Phineas over issues unknown to the rest of us, but crucial to the future of the world, if their facial expressions were any indication. Antidrug and alcohol posters were everywhere. A kid couldn't run even the shortest sprint race without sailing past at least a couple of SAY NO messages. Emmett must have been in seventh heaven; probably never in the history of the town had the people of Wakefield had their attention so solidly focused on so many convenient ways to mess up their lives.

I had just set down my end of a table and turned back to the truck containing the rest of the tables when I felt myself wrapped in a bear hug. "It's coming off, man," Emmett said, flushed with the kind of exhausted warmth and goodwill you expect in the closing moments of a thirty-six hour telethon. "It's really coming off!"

He was gone before I had a chance to say anything, which was probably just as well. Why not let the guy have his big moment.

Pop didn't make it until almost six. He'd sent Ethan over earlier, saying he could manage in the office alone this one time. When Pop finally arrived, Ethan and I showed him around before we sat down to eat. Actually, Ethan did most of the showing, pointing out all the different booths and all the different games we'd played and whether or not we'd won anything at them. I was still keeping a pretty sharp lookout for Katie. I almost had the feeling that if I saw her (and she saw me), she'd recognize me as the guy who'd worked so tirelessly on her behalf against her parents that whole afternoon, and her face would light up with a shy smile. But I didn't see her, and I figured more than ever she must be away, spending the weekend with her father.

We were just finishing up eating when Rosasharn and Jeremy came up to our table. Rosasharn, after bowing dramatically and saying, "O kind and distinguished father of the great and not-too-shabby Riley clan" and on like that, asked Pop if he and Jeremy could borrow Ethan for a little while. Pop roared through the whole routine like he always does during a Rosasharn performance, and then said that if Ethan was agreeable to the idea, they were certainly most welcome to his good company. I didn't have a clue as to what Rosasharn was up to or why he needed Ethan, and I didn't give it much thought. I'd long ago decided that trying to speculate about the day-to-day workings of a brain that vibrated at his particular frequency just wasn't worth the effort.

I watched as the three of them disappeared into the crowd and then asked Pop if he felt like heading up toward the bonfire behind the school. It was when we were strolling up the hill that I spotted Katie. At first it didn't register with me that it was really her. I'd seen so much of her lately in my mind's eye that it took my brain a few seconds to grasp that she actually *was* there. When it did, my brain went into overload, leaving me light-headed and slack-jawed. She was with Heather Lutz, and they were just hanging there halfway up the slope as if they were waiting for somebody. As we ambled by them, I could feel Heather giving me the once-over, and then she gave a not-so-subtle jab to Katie. I think Katie looked over, but I can't be sure. As soon as I thought her eyes might be heading my way, my eyes went for the ground. I could've kicked myself for that, but it was an involuntary thing, like flinching when you first spot a snake.

"*Ladies*," I heard Pop say and I could picture just the kind of little bow he'd give them, "you're looking lovely as usual. I hope you're enjoying the evening."

"Oh, hi, Mr. Riley. Yes, we are. Thanks." Both of them kind of answered at once, so it was hard to tell who said what, especially since my eyes were still busy studying the grass. The fact that Katie seemed to know Pop shouldn't have surprised me as much as it did since practically everybody in the whole town does. I think in some sense I hadn't come to the full realization yet that she truly did exist outside my mental realm, and the fact that her physical existence somehow intersected with mine caught me a little off guard.

I waited until we'd moseyed a little further up the hill and Pop had already greeted two or three other groups of people before I said anything.

"How well do you know Katie Lyons's family, Pop?"

"We go back a ways," he told me. "I've known Mike and Allison for a good long while—since before they were married as a matter of fact."

"But they're divorced now, huh?"

"Heavens, no," Pop said, sounding a little surprised. "They've remained one of the closest families it's ever been my privilege to know. And that Katie . . ." He paused and nodded his head thoughtfully. "As far as her parents are concerned, the sun absolutely rises and shines for that girl."

Well, I thought, seeing my afternoon's rescue work going up in smoke, at least I was right about one thing.

It had just turned dark when it happened. We'd finally made it to the bonfire where, since just before sunset, the little kids had been gathering and staking out seats down in front where the ghost stories would be told. Of course they had to pay for that privilege by first sitting through a series of peer leadership activities which, among other things, included the obligatory mock beer party skit—you know, the one where a kid who doesn't want to drink is being harassed by other kids whose only purpose in life seems to be to get him to do it. The peer leaders playing the drinkers hammed it up for a good ten minutes, riding the non-drinking kid without mercy until finally, accompanied by cheers from some junior high kids at the back, he popped open a tall one. The cheers from the back were not part of the official program. Neither was the "pfft" sound Pop made as he opened a beer of his own, leaning over and explaining to me that all that talk about drinking made a person thirsty. I had the feeling there was some wisdom in that statement that had eluded the planning committee.

Next came the postskit discussion, designed to get the little kids to tell how they'd never fall for that kind of peer pressure. The whole thing was pretty bizarre—especially considering that Bo was the only peer leader up there who didn't drink himself, and everybody knew it.

After all the peer pressure skits and assorted malarky, the kids got what they were *really* there for: Mr. Woodman's ghost stories. Mr. Woodman was a teacher in the middle school and a professional storyteller on the side. For my money, he was a little overly dramatic, with his bulging eyes and his alternately booming and then hushed voice, but younger kids really eat that stuff up. He told all the usual yarns like the one about the escaped mental patient with a hook for a hand who had hidden out in a rain forest just outside of town (it didn't matter that the nearest rain forest was probably in Costa Rica), and how a guy and a girl who were parking there one night got spooked by a noise outside their car, and peeled out of there, only to discover a bloody hook hanging from the door handle when they got to the girl's house. He followed with a couple of generic ghost stories before moving on to his grand finale—stories about our own Blood Red Pond swamp creature. His stories about this swamp monster had grown over the years, and he knew just when to lower his voice for effect and when to pause and say "Hark" and to look bulgy-eyed out into the dark woods. He was doing a decent job on this night, even for my tastes, and it's ironic that I had just been feeling a little sorry that Ethan was missing the performance when it happened. Mr. Woodman was in the middle of his best swamp monster story and had done the "hark" business and was staring into the woods when all hell broke loose. First we heard a god-awful cry come from right where he was staring, and then out of the woods charged not one, but *three* creatures of the night.

If anybody there had kept his head, it wouldn't have been hard to see that these particular creatures of the night were pretty low-budget, not to mention exactly the same size and shape as Rosasharn and Jeremy and Ethan. But it all happened so fast and the little kids were going crazy knocking chairs over and crawling over each other to get as far away from the monsters as possible that nobody had time to think. One of the reasons the kids believed these creatures were the real thing was that Mr. Woodman's exaggerated fear-face scaled itself back to a look of genuine shock and for once in his life he gave the kind of understated performance that real people give in real situations. I looked over and saw Pop staring slack-jawed at the three creatures charging past the bonfire. Kids were already streaming around us, heading like an old-fashioned cattle stampede down the hill toward where most of their parents were still sitting around at the tables on the football field.

"It's Ethan," I managed to say to Pop as he was giving the label on his current beer a second take. "It's Ethan, Rosasharn, and Jeremy." I pointed them out as best I could, considering the confusion.

Pop isn't slow to catch on to things. No sooner had the words sunk into his head than his puzzled expression transformed itself into the most undiluted smile I'd ever seen on him, without even a hint of sadness lurking anywhere. At just that moment I spotted Katie over Pop's shoulder on the other side of the crowd of stampeding kids, her hand up to her mouth, her dark eyes taking in first the swamp creatures, then Heather, and then going back for another stare at the swamp creatures. I'd never seen her look more beautiful.

What followed ranks right up there with the greatest moments of my life so far. There was Katie off in the distance, looking more lovely and mysterious than ever in the flickering firelight, and yet so vulnerable it made my heart ache. And there was Pop, as happy as I'd ever seen him, practically dancing with joy and howling like some raspy-voiced kid. "Ethan," he was saying whenever he could catch his breath enough to say anything. "God bless him! Our little Ethan!" And there was Ethan. I couldn't see his face, but the way he ran and the little trademark aloha wave he gave as he passed by us said it all. He was having the time of his life.

I'll never forget how I felt at that moment. It was the closest I've ever come to experiencing pure happiness with nothing else mixed in. I had no way of knowing that events were already starting to happen that would soon put a damper on things, but even if I'd known, I don't think it would have clouded the way I felt then. It was *that* pure.

Ten

I heard about Mr. Lindstrom the next morning. I'd stayed overnight at Bo's house and Pop called around eight to break the news to me. He didn't know many details—just that Walter Owens had been driving by on his way to Stewart's for his morning coffee and had seen Mr. Lindstrom's pickup truck parked in front of his old barn with the barn door wide open. Nothing so strange in that, except Walter had seen the truck parked in exactly the same spot with the barn door open exactly the same way the night before. Walter thought at the time it was a little odd that Mr. Lindstrom would be out working around his property after dark, but didn't give it another thought until he saw a carbon copy of the scene the next morning, and decided to swing back to check on things. That's when he found Mr. Lindstrom, lying face up a couple hundred feet down the lane. He was alive—but just barely—and the rescue squad had come and rushed him off to Mary McClellan Hospital in Cambridge. That was all Pop knew.

I didn't show any big reaction to the news; I just stood listening quietly as Pop explained the situation. But I felt like I'd been punched in the stomach. I couldn't believe it. Right up until Pop called I'd been having one of the best mornings I'd had in a long time. I woke up around six with a pretty decent afterglow from the previous evening. While Bo meditated, I did a five-mile run in the cool morning air, smiling every time I thought about Ethan and the attack of the swamp creatures and what a charge Pop had gotten out of the whole thing. I smiled some more, but in a different way, when I thought about how mysterious and beautiful Katie had looked standing there in the glow of the bonfire. As I was heading back up to Bo's room I could hear Mr. and Mrs. Michaelson bouncing around in their basement, and that made me smile too. Every bounce they took seemed like a bubble of hope, a promise of good things to come, and the feathery lightness of that promise seemed to pervade the entire house. Anyway, things that morning were looking bright, and by the time I climbed out of Bo's shower, feeling all clean and good, the last thing I expected was bad news. Then Pop called and told me about Mr. Lindstrom.

It's not that Mr. Lindstrom and I had ever been that close. Mr. Lindstrom wasn't the kind of person anybody got close to, even if you *were* one of the few people he liked. He'd always been somewhat of a mystery to me and I sometimes wondered if he might even be a little crazy, although *crazy* is one of those words that's almost impossible to define, and I tend to wonder more about regular people—the ones who do and say pretty much everything that's expected of them, and you have to ask yourself what's really going on upstairs there. Still, Mr. Lindstrom had been known to do some unusual things. At night sometimes, if we were outside and the sound was carrying just right, we used to hear him over at his place yelling at the top of his lungs and blasting his car horn for all he was worth. The first few times we heard it, we went over to check on him—Pop and I the first time, and Bo and I the second—and both times he'd looked a little relieved when he saw it was us and insisted we come in and stay for a while. Neither time did he let on that anything out of the ordinary had been going on. Pop figured he was lonely—*that* and a little paranoid, two things he said went together more than most people realized—and that shouting and blowing his car horn may simply have been his way of whistling in the dark.

The next couple of times we heard him start to carry on like that Ethan and I sneaked onto the hill across the road from his house and crouched down there to watch. Twice Mr. Lindstrom came charging out of his house and ran to his car yelling things like "Leave me be, ya bastards!" then blowing his horn some and charging back into the house. He had his yard light on that night, and from where we were watching, the yard looked like a lighted stage showcasing a one-man show. That's the reason I didn't feel worse for him than I did, I think, because he seemed so much like an actor playing out some kind of bizarre role.

I felt plenty bad about it after Pop called, though, and as Bo drove me to my house I couldn't help thinking about how, except for us, Mr. Lindstrom was virtually alone in the world, and for the last few years at least, he must have been afraid a lot of the time and had to resort to carrying on and shouting threats at whatever it was he imagined might be lurking out there in the darkness. It made me sad, and I wished I had taken more time to visit him.

When we got to my house, Pop was on the phone trying to reach Mr. Lindstrom's daughter. The last I'd heard anything about her she was living someplace in Maryland. I'd never laid eyes on her myself; she'd been estranged from her father for years over some falling-out they'd had that I'd never gotten the particulars on.

Mr. Lindstrom's only other child, a son, had been killed in a car accident returning home from Saratoga late one night on a long straight stretch of road we called the Schuylerville Flats. He'd been celebrating his eighteenth birthday. People claimed Mr. Lindstrom never quite got over that and started to keep more to himself and get more peculiar from then on, and that it only got worse after his wife died and his daughter left. I knew he missed his daughter because Pop once told me that after she left, he'd buy presents every Christmas and on her birthday and wrap them and send them to her. And every time they were returned unopened. One year he even had Pop get him a private investigator to find her new address. He finally located her, but it didn't do any good. The presents were returned the same as before. After that, I guess he gave up.

I couldn't tell who Pop got through to, but it wasn't her because he explained the whole story (or as much of it as he knew) and asked if the person would be kind enough to see that she was notified. Then he gave our number and arranged to have his calls forwarded to the hospital, where he and Ethan were heading to check on Mr. Lindstrom. Meanwhile, he wondered if Bo and I would mind going over to Mr. Lindstrom's place to check on things and make sure the doors were locked and the windows were closed and all that. We always left our own doors unlocked, but someone was always coming and going from our place, and that was different from leaving a house completely abandoned, especially when the whole town would soon know the place was vacant. I couldn't help but wonder as we headed over there, if Mr. Lindstrom didn't make it (and Pop had warned me that it didn't look good), who we were protecting the property *for*. From what I'd heard about the daughter, she wouldn't want to have anything to do with her father *or* his property. The whole idea of it made me feel worse than I already did.

Mr. Lindstrom's house was on the south side of Blood Red Pond and sat quite a ways back from the road in the middle of what was now a hayfield. His place always struck me as looking like it belonged in Kansas or Nebraska or someplace like that, where you often see old abandoned houses sitting smack-dab in the middle of huge wheat fields. It was a good-sized house, yellow with a flat roof and a bunch of curlicue buttresses that were used to support the overhang and embellish things. That effect may have worked in its day, but ever since I can remember the house has looked pretty sad, sitting there marooned in the field like that, needing paint and other basic repairs, with no yard to speak of, only a small unkempt area out in front with a few scraggly bushes and an old box elder, which is what you might call the tree version of a weed and didn't add any kind of homey quality to the place. Just looking around the yard made me sadder still.

The long driveway curved around in front of the house and became the other end of the lane that went to the pond and then back out to the road by the old barn we'd hid in the night Rosasharn jumped on Ray's car. You could see the woods where the pond sat at the upper end of the hayfield about a quarter mile away. The pond itself sat quite a ways back in the woods and was probably as close to our house as it was to Mr. Lindstrom's.

We went to the back door, and I fished the key Pop had given me out of my pocket. I stood there with my hand on the knob for a few seconds before opening it. I was almost wishing Jeremy was there. He probably would have grumbled something sarcastic and pushed me through, and I would have fired a suitable insult back and maybe punched him, and it might have helped bring my mood back to normal.

What hit me first, even before I had the door open all the way, was the smell. I could never quite identify what made Mr. Lindstrom's house smell the way it did—probably because there was no one cause for it. He was no housekeeper, and there were always empty tuna fish cans and things lying around and dirty dishes on his kitchen table and in his sink, but somehow they didn't totally explain the smell because no matter what day you went there, and no matter what kinds of cans were lying around or what was on the dirty dishes or in the garbage, the smell was always the same. It was thick and acrid, permeating the whole house and by no means pleasant. Eventually the place would probably have to be fumigated.

When I stepped into the kitchen, I saw the same living-alone-old-guy kind of mess I'd come to expect from that house, and then some. There wasn't a clean anything anywhere, and that made me sad too. I noticed that his Mr. Coffee was still on. It must have been one of the older models without the automatic shutoff. All the water had evaporated away, leaving the coffee baked to the bottom of the pot. I pulled it off the heating pad, put some water in it, and set it by the sink next to the other dirty dishes to let it soak. The next thing I knew I'd dug out some Dawn and was washing the dishes in the sink. Don't ask me why. It's not something I'd normally even think to do, let alone do without thinking. Bo started clearing off the table and counters and washing them down with a cloth. Then he grabbed a broom and swept the floor. Somewhere along the line he must have opened the window in front of the sink because all of a sudden I was aware of a fresh breeze coming in from the outside world. Neither of us had said anything the whole time.

Twenty minutes later the kitchen was pretty well taken care of, looking better than I'd ever seen it, although the smell still lingered, even with the window open. We had just moved on to the living room when Jeremy and Rosasharn and Sudie arrived. They walked in awkwardly, not knowing quite how to act or what to say in the living room of a person who might at that very moment be dying. Rosasharn wasn't being the clown and Jeremy wasn't being the crank, and that left a little bit of a vacuum there, at least for me.

Sudie pitched in first, finding a cloth and dusting the coffee table and the TV and the old fireplace mantel, with its knickknacks and photos dating back to when the Lindstroms were a family. Jeremy and Rosasharn found some Windex and started in on the windows, which from the looks of them hadn't had any major contact with that Windex for a good long while.

Before noon we had the whole downstairs taken care of, including the bathroom, and the less said about *that*, the better. I'd thought about tackling the upstairs too, but there's something about the upstairs of a house that seems more private, and even though I was curious because I'd never seen it, I didn't feel as if we should intrude. Maybe if it'd been only Bo and me instead of all five of us, I'd have felt different. I don't know.

Before we left, I walked over to the big wooden mantel and looked at the old family pictures. The first was a wedding picture, and it seemed to have been taken out in front of the house. I recognized Mr. Lindstrom right away, standing stiffly and looking so out of place in his tuxedo. Back then he was a big bear of a guy, and I thought again how he reminded me a little of the plowman in the Icarus painting Bo had made for Ethan. His wife wore a frilly white wedding gown and was smiling shyly into the camera. She was kind of pretty, and looked so thin and delicate next to her husband. The next picture was of two little kids, a girl of about six who was scowling into the camera and a boy of three or four who was peeking out from under a Yankees hat. Next to those were what looked like their senior pictures. The thing that struck me right away was how different the son and the daughter were, which, I realized after a while, was the exact same difference as between Mr. Lindstrom and his wife. There was no question that the son took after his mother, and the daughter was the spitting image of her father, which, for a girl, was definitely not a good thing. She and her father both had big heads and coarse features and both looked like if they smiled their faces would crack. The boy had a more sensitive face, like the mother, and even from the senior picture you could tell he had her slight build too. I studied his picture some more. I knew he'd been killed during his senior year, so it couldn't have happened too long after that picture was taken. I couldn't help wondering what he was like. I didn't wonder about the daughter. For some reason I felt as if I already had a pretty good idea what she was like.

Pop called just as I was locking up. When he hadn't been able to reach me at home, he figured I might still be at Mr. Lindstrom's. The news wasn't all bad, but it wasn't very good either. Mr. Lindstrom had suffered a fairly serious stroke, and his entire left side was paralyzed. He was conscious—at least somewhat—but he still couldn't speak, and the doctors had no way of knowing if he'd ever make it up and around again. As you might guess, he wasn't a very good patient, and with the little capacity to move that he had, he was flailing around and giving the nurses an awful time. Nobody could tell what it was he was trying to tell them, but my guess was that at least part of it contained the phrase "sons-o'-bitches." The doctors had given him something to calm him down and now he was resting comfortably. Pop was taking Ethan to lunch at the Cambridge Hotel, and then they were going to check at the hospital again to see how Mr. Lindstrom was doing.

On the way back to my house Bo and I stopped to lock up Mr. Lindstrom's barn. I didn't want his boat or tools or anything to end up stolen. You could still see the tracks from where the ambulance had strayed off the lane as it backed in to pick him up. Pop had heard right: Mr. Lindstrom had collapsed a couple hundred feet down the lane. That's where the tracks stopped.

"I wonder why he opened the barn door and then walked over to there," I said to Bo. "He always opened the door to get the tractor or bulldozer out, and then he'd close it and lock it right behind him. *Always.*"

Bo shrugged. "Maybe he walked out to clear a branch off the lane or something. There's always dead wood falling off those old maple trees."

"Yeah, maybe." I walked into the barn and looked around. Everything seemed pretty much the way it should have been, with not so much as a gas can out of place. I was starting to feel a little foolish about playing the TV detective when something caught my eye. I don't know how I could have noticed it from halfway across the barn, but I did. I walked over to the tractor for a closer look. "That's strange," I yelled over to Bo. "The key is on."

Bo walked over to where I was. "You think it wouldn't start for him when he tried it?"

"Could be." I climbed up and tried the key. The starter clicked a few times, but that was it. "The battery's dead—at least it is now. . . ." I flicked off the key and thought. Then I leaned out over the hood, pulled off the gas cap, and looked down inside. "It started all right," I said. "And it sat here running until it ran out of gas."

"Or it wouldn't start *because* it was out of gas," Bo offered.

I shook my head. "You're thinking about people like us. Mr. Lindstrom never let his tank get anywhere near empty. He checked every fluid level every day before he started working. He must've started the tractor up, left it sitting there running, and *then* went down the lane for some reason."

I wondered about that for a while but didn't come up with anything. Then I forgot about it—at least until a few more strange things started happening that made me think about it some more.

Eleven

The next school week blew by at a decent clip—starting with two days of last-minute review in classes with exams that meant something and wasting time in those that didn't. Local exams began on Wednesday and state Regents exams the following Monday. I wasn't a last-minute study-er (some teachers might say I was no kind of study-er), but I paid attention in class and read most of the assigned readings, which was more than a lot of the kids did, so I wasn't worried. There would always be a few kids like Bo who'd score higher, but that didn't bother me. I knew I'd end up with a halfway-decent average.

There was quite a bit of talk about the infamous raid of the drug field day by the mystery creatures, but as far as I could tell nobody took it all that seriously. There was a small mention of it in the *Post Star*, but it was largely treated as a prank, not as some kind of supernatural visitation. After school on Monday Ethan told me that Mrs. Quinby had been around to all the elementary and middle school classrooms to talk about the raid and to tell the kids that it was all right to be afraid. I could just picture her swooping around, hoping to find even a flicker of an emotional response, so she could fan that flicker into a flame. Ethan said that by the end of the day she'd rounded up a whole flock of kids, many of whom hadn't even *been* at the field day. They ended up taking over the elementary library to begin the healing process. Even Ethan thought that was funny. He was wearing a big smile all while he was telling me about it.

Of course we all stayed mum about who was responsible for the attack, even Pop, who claimed it would be a shame to destroy the "delicious mystery of the thing." I was glad because I didn't want Ray McPherson putting two and two together and coming after us. What I didn't know was that Ray was *already* putting two and two together, but being the kind of mathematician he was, he wasn't coming up with four. I learned that later. At the time my mind was on other things. I'd been kept pretty busy running back and forth to the hospital with Pop, and whenever I had a free moment, I only wanted to kick back, dream of Katie, and savor the winding down of the school year.

Jeremy was one of the kids who couldn't afford to do any kicking back, dreaming, or savoring. In addition to being reasonably unprepared for all of his exams, he was in real danger of failing social studies, with or without the exam, because of a research paper he'd turned in about the Nazis—without going to the trouble of doing any research on the Nazis. Knowing Jeremy, he probably got most of his information from watching old episodes of *Hogan's Heroes.*

Tuesday evening Jeremy was bringing his lame paper over to Bo's for help in overhauling it. I didn't want to miss out on that so I had Pop drop me off at the Michaelsons' on the way back from the hospital.

When Jeremy arrived I resisted the temptation to run up and snatch the paper out of his hands. He knew what a kick I got out of his papers, and that was one of the reasons he'd asked Bo for help and not me. It's not that I thought Jeremy was stupid. When it came to certain things, he was smarter than I'd ever be. He could tear down an engine, fix it, and put it back together quicker and better than most professional mechanics, and he's intelligent to talk to—when he wants to be. But academically, forget it. The things he writes on paper, and even his handwriting itself, are so innocent and childlike, they never fail to crack me up.

Anyway, when Jeremy walked into Bo's room, I just sat there and continued looking at the book I had in my hands. Bo was down in the den finishing his evening meditation so I had some time to play with.

"Hi, scrub," Jeremy said finally when I didn't even look up.

"Oh, hi," I said, acting kind of surprised to see him.

I kept my face in the book while Jeremy scrounged around the room for a while. He was the worst when it came to scrounging through other people's things, picking stuff up and examining it, snooping through drawers and like that. It drove me crazy when he did it in my room, but Bo was used to it and didn't mind. Jeremy's scrounge rounds in Bo's room were fairly short-lived anyway, since he was already so familiar with everything there, and pretty soon he settled down in a chair and started looking through his research paper, which he'd been holding on to all while he was scrounging. I still held back. Jeremy's the impatient type, and I knew if I waited him out, it was only a matter of time before I'd have the paper in my hands.

"I can't believe DeFablo's making me do this over," he said finally.

"He's tough on papers," I lied.

"It's the last week of school and all he's worried about is this stupid paper."

"What'd he say was wrong with it?" I said it casually and didn't even look up from my book.

Jeremy grunted. "What *didn't* he say was wrong with it?"

I shook my head in mild commiseration and went back to my book. It took about half a minute, but then Jeremy got up and headed my way.

"Look at it," he said. "It's not that bad." Being as impatient as he was, he kind of batted me in the face with it and then held it out for me.

I looked up at the paper. It was right in front of my eyes, but I played it cool and didn't reach for it or anything.

"Look at it," Jeremy said, batting me in the face one more time. He plopped the paper down on my lap.

I gave the kind of sigh tired parents give to nagging kids and then picked up the paper. The trick now would be to keep a straight face while reading it. One smile and I knew he'd snatch it back. I screwed on a serious look and started in:

> *The Germans hated the Jews. They hated the Jews because they thought they were cheep.*

That was as far as I got. The whole idea was ridiculous enough, but it was the word "cheep" sitting there at the end of the second sentence that did me in. All I could think of was this old *I Love Lucy* episode where Ethel told Fred these baby chicks were talking about him because they kept saying, "Cheep, cheep, cheep." No matter how hard I tried I couldn't keep the smile off my face.

Jeremy, who'd been watching me like an attack dog, snatched the paper out of my hand so fast I was lucky I didn't get some kind of life-threatening paper cut. "Shut up," he said, even though I hadn't said anything yet.

When Bo walked in a few minutes later, I had

Jeremy on the floor trying to wrestle the paper out of his hands. "I must see more," I said, pretending to be a crazed zombie. "You mustn't keep me from that paper!"

"Get off me, you jerk!" Jeremy said, swatting at me.

"I see you've already started working on the paper," Bo said.

"'The Germans hated the Jews'" I quoted. "'They hated the Jews because they thought they were *cheep*'— C-H-E-E-P."

"They *did*," Jeremy said, giving me one last cuff to the head. "I remember learning it." He looked to Bo, who was wearing a big smile, more than likely at the entire scene and not just about Jews being "cheep." "Tell 'im," Jeremy demanded.

"I know what you meant," Bo said judiciously. "Hitler did accuse the Jews of controlling too much money and of ruining the German economy."

"*Face*," Jeremy said, leering my way. "In your face!"

I laughed. "You're telling me that what *you* said is the same as what he just said?" A better person might have felt a little ashamed that Bo, who was half Jewish himself, was being so much nicer than I was, but I didn't. Not too much anyway. For one thing, Bo was *always* nicer than I was and I was pretty much used to it, and for another, the shoe had been on the other foot enough times that picking on Jeremy didn't exactly feel like picking on some innocent babe in the woods.

"It's the same thing," Jeremy said. "He just explained it more."

"All right," I said, getting to my feet. "Okay, I admit it. It's the same thing." I reached a hand down to help Jeremy up. "So are you gonna let me see the rest of it?"

Now it was Jeremy who was smiling—in his Jeremy sort of way. "Uh-uh," he said, shaking his head, "If I let

you read it, you'll probably end up thinking Hitler is supposed to stand for that what's-her-face lady."

"Mrs. Quinby," Bo told him helpfully.

"Yeah," Jeremy sneered.

Wednesday evening after dinner, Ethan and I headed out on our bikes. Ethan had actually found a beaver
dam while he was wandering around the afternoon
before and he was eager to show it to me. To be honest,
after all the searching we'd done for beavers in the last
couple of years, it was kind of anticlimactic to know I
was about to see some, which I all of a sudden seemed
to remember were actually members of the rodent family. Ethan was pretty excited, though, so I acted that way
too. That afternoon I'd taken my first final—English,
which I was pretty sure I'd aced—and since all my other
exams were Regents, which were given the following
week, I had the rest of the week off. I figured I'd probably end up doing some studying, especially for biology,
but I didn't see any need to rush into things.

It was almost twilight when we got as close to
where we were going as we could on our bikes, and we
ditched them and set off through the woods.

"There's a whole family of them," Ethan said right
before we got to the stream. These were his first words
since we'd left the house, but I knew he'd been thinking
about those beavers all the way there. A few seconds
later as we cleared the crest of the last knoll, he touched
my elbow and pointed. There was the dam, strung out
across the stream and holding back enough water so it
was building up behind it and flooding out over the
banks. In the center of the pool of water that had col-
lected behind the dam was the lodge, sitting there like a
collapsed wigwam. Ethan showed me the pointed

stumps of some saplings the beavers had chewed down, and then we sat on the side hill and watched to see if any beavers were out and around. There didn't seem to be much doing down there, which didn't surprise me since it was so late. I was about to tell Ethan I was afraid we were out of luck when I felt him touch my elbow again. A dark shape moved across the water and did a surface dive to enter the lodge. You could tell it was a beaver by the way it moved. We waited to see if any other beavers were going to make an appearance.

"I think they're all tucked in for the night, Ethe," I said after a while.

We still sat there. It was so peaceful that neither of us was in any hurry to leave.

"I used to think that all the animals in the forest were really friends," Ethan said a few minutes later. That's the way Ethan was—coming up with things like that right out of the blue—but the funny thing was, when he did it, I'd almost always know exactly what he was talking about.

"Remember *Mr. Bear Builds His House*?" he asked me.

I smiled. I knew that's what he'd been thinking of. Pop used to read that book to me when I was little, and we both used to read it to Ethan. In the story all the animals in the forest showed up to help Mr. Bear build a log cabin, and the beavers did more than anybody. "Remember how the beavers cut down all the trees for the bear?" I said.

Ethan nodded. "And then when the walls were up, they used their tails to smear mud between the cracks to keep the wind out."

We sat there for a while without saying anything. I don't know how, but I could tell Ethan was really thinking hard about something.

"Do you think we ever really believed it?" he said

finally. "You know, that all those animals really got along and helped each other?"

I thought about it. "I did, I think. Maybe not that they got along every minute, but that they were friends. I think I believed *that.*"

Ethan's face was serious, even for him, as he tried to get what he was thinking to come out right. "The thing with me is, even when I felt like I believed it, I still knew it wasn't true. I mean, we'd always watch those nature shows on TV where animals were fighting and eating each other all the time. And, remember, Mr. Lindstrom had that dog Sheila who'd go around killing woodchucks every day. She didn't even eat them or anything. She'd just catch them and kill them, one after the other." He stopped and looked at me. "It's just funny—you know— how you can believe something and still know it's not true."

Sometimes I thought Ethan must be quite a bit smarter than I ever was. He was always coming up with those kinds of things that I'd never thought of.

"Is that the way it is with Superman, do you think?" I'd often wondered just how seriously Ethan took that whole Superman business, but I'd never come right out and asked him before.

He nodded. "Kind of. I know there's nobody who flies around in a cape saving people and all that. But it's still *kind* of true. There *are* people who save people. Like Pop does in court. And the flying part—Mr. and Mrs. Michaelson kind of do that. One of these days, I bet they'll take right off. Don't ya think?"

I sort of shrugged and nodded at the same time. It's not that I believed they wouldn't; it's just that I didn't believe they *would.* But I hated to tell Ethan that. He'd always been fascinated by the idea of the Michaelsons going into their basement and doing their flying practice twice a day—a lot more fascinated than I'd ever been. I liked it, but I took it pretty much for granted, the way you do TV or radio or fax machines—the kind of things that really *are* kind of amazing, but when you've grown up with them you don't give them much thought. With Ethan it was different; if something was amazing, it was amazing, and that was that.

"I think they will," Ethan said. "I'd bet anything they will." He was looking at me to see what my reaction would be. "And when I get older," he continued, "I'm gonna do it too. I'm gonna sign up for the same course Mr. and Mrs. Michaelson took, and I'm gonna keep practicing every day till I fly." He had his jaw set and he was studying me, probably to see if I'd smile or anything. It reminded me of the way Jeremy had watched me when he gave me his Nazi paper to read, and I felt a little bad.

"Learning to fly would be pretty cool," I said after a while. "Maybe I'll sign up for that course with you."

Ethan didn't say anything more. But he put his hand on my shoulder as we looked down over the beaver dam.

It was almost dark by the time we came into view of Mr. Lindstrom's place. We were moving right along, trying to make it home while we could still see the road, when Ethan all of a sudden stopped in front of me. I almost rear-ended him. I looked up and saw him staring out across the field. It took me a few seconds to figure out what he was staring at. I mean it wasn't hard to see that he was looking at Mr. Lindstrom's house, but what for? Then it dawned on me. It was such a common everyday sight I didn't even notice it at first, but when I did, I felt a little chill go up my spine. Upstairs, in one of the rooms that faced the road, a light was on.

Twelve

I didn't make it back to check on Mr. Lindstrom's house until late Friday night. Ethan and I didn't have a key with us the night we first saw the light, so we'd continued on home. And then after I'd had time to think about it, that light being on didn't seem so strange. We'd never gone upstairs on the day we cleaned the place. And even though I'd been up and down the road a bunch of times since then, it had always been daylight and I wouldn't have noticed it anyway. I figured Mr. Lindstrom had probably left the light on himself, before the stroke. Not only that, but I started thinking that having a light on might actually be a good thing, giving the impression that someone was staying there and cutting down on the chances of a break-in.

Even with the exams coming up the following week, I had a pretty strong feeling that for me the summer had started. I love summer. Except for a couple of too hot days each year, I love everything about it: the sunshine, the thunderstorms, the long evenings, you name it. But the best thing, as far as I'm concerned, is waking up in the morning and getting to decide what you *want* to do that day, not simply marching through the day doing all the things you have to do. I knew this might be my last real "kid" summer because, next time around, I'd be sixteen and I'd have to try to land at least some kind of regular job—something more steady than just helping out on the Wulfsons' farm when they needed me or fiddling around at Rosa's with Sudie and Rosasharn. I've never minded working, but I wasn't crazy about the idea of tying up big chunks of time. Even without a regular job, I can never find enough time to do all the things I want to do.

On Thursday Bo and I took The Tank to Rensselaer and caught the train to New York. At least two or three times a year we'd make a point to go to the Museum of Television and Radio on Fifty-second Street, where we'd get to watch old TV shows we couldn't see anyplace else. After hanging out there for a while we wandered around checking out different stores and then taking in a movie we'd read about that wasn't showing upstate.

That evening we watched the sun go down over the city from the top of the World Trade Center, and it was after midnight before we got home. A few times during the day I caught myself thinking about how nice it would be to be in New York with Katie. Not that I wasn't having a good time with Bo, but being there with Katie would have been like something out of a dream. *Someday,* I thought, and couldn't help but smile. I smiled too when I thought about having all of July and August stretched out in front of me like a blank canvas just waiting for all kinds of good things to be put down on it.

Bo had the next day off too, and we decided to go to the old Rexleigh covered bridge outside Salem. I think a combination of things put that idea into my head. First, it had been a long winter and I was eager to revisit all my old favorite swimming spots. I may have thought of this particular one first because of Ethan putting beavers on my brain, and that was the place where the summer before a kid had actually been attacked by a beaver while swimming and his mother had to beat the thing off his back. Also, I was starting to think it might be a good place to bring Katie. Maybe that seems strange—thinking about bringing a girl you practically worship and haven't even asked out yet to swim at the site of an unprovoked beaver attack, but when I got to thinking about the other kinds of swimming spots where I could bring her, the options seemed limited. There was a quarry outside of town, but that was the kind of place where kids went to drink and fight—not to mention that it was illegal to be there, and Katie didn't seem like the type who would appreciate being arrested on a first or second date. The cliffs in Schaghticoke were spectacular for daredevil diving, but they weren't as good for just hanging around and swimming and talking. The covered bridge just seemed right—it was a wholesome family kind of place, like something you'd see in a Grandma Moses painting, which wasn't surprising since Grandma Moses hadn't lived that far from there. I figured Katie would love it.

The covered bridge had a few boards missing—deliberately missing, most likely, so you could dive off the side. I've always found the quick plunge to be the best way to get wet, so I headed up to the bridge. Bo was right there with me. As far as I could tell, no one else was around.

"You think that beaver thing hurt the crowds here?" As I said this, I was leaning out through the gap in the boards, checking for any signs of beavers guarding the place.

"Maybe," Bo said. "I read that when *Jaws* first came out in theaters, a lot of people were afraid to go into the ocean."

"Yeah," I said. "I still think about that whenever

I'm on Martha's Vineyard." I looked around some more. "You know, we could do that whole *Jaws* thing here, but do it with a beaver instead of a shark. As kind of a spoof."

Bo laughed. "Remember *Piranha?*"

"Oh, yeah," I said. "Wasn't it *Piranha* where that fish came sailing out of the water and clamped itself onto that guy's face? You really can't go too wrong with flying attack fish." I took off my sneakers and tossed them out over the water and onto the shore where we'd stashed the rest of our stuff. Then I looked back inside the bridge at Bo. "For my money though, the Big Daddy of all goofy horror films is still *Killdozer.* That film *rules.*" Bo and I had always had this thing for bad films—we loved them almost as much as the great ones. When we were younger and staying over at each other's houses, we'd always go through the TV listings trying to see who could find the best worst late-night film. We both claimed credit for *Killdozer.*

Bo pulled off his sneakers and nodded. "Another sure thing—a bulldozer with an attitude."

"*And* Fess Parker," I added.

"*Wrong,*" Bo said. "Fess Parker was the guy who played Davy Crockett. Clint Walker was the guy in *Killdozer.*"

I was about to argue the point but decided not to. Bo was almost always right when it came to that kind of thing. "Have it your way," I said as if I was doing him some big favor. Then, stepping out through the gap in the side of the bridge, I did one last beaver check. "Well, here goes nothing."

Two seconds later I realized it may not have been beavers that were keeping the crowds away. That water was *cold.* I'd forgotten just how cold the

Battenkill could be. All that water was runoff from the mountains of Vermont, and it went a long way toward explaining how they could have such a long ski season there.

Bo hit the water right after I did, and his reaction was the same as mine. We both hightailed it for land.

"This was your idea, I think," Bo said after we climbed out of the water.

"It seemed good in theory," I said, grabbing my towel and handing Bo his.

We dried off as fast as we could and put our shirts and sneakers back on and then lay out in the sun for a while trying to soak up some heat. Then we grabbed Bo's camera bag out of The Tank, figuring as long as we were there we should get some file footage of the bridge and the Battenkill and the surrounding area. We already had some footage from the previous fall, but in early June the place had a whole different look. Plus, it might not be that deserted again for the rest of the season. Over the years we'd stockpiled tons of footage from different places and never passed up a chance to get more. We never knew when we'd need some of it for establishing shots. These are the shots you use to show where your scene is supposedly taking place—like in *The Beverly Hillbillies* when they'll show you the front of the huge mansion and then cut to a scene in the kitchen. The thing *is,* the kitchen isn't even *in* the mansion, but everyone watching believes it is. A good filmmaker is a little like a magician; he knows that what you see is what you *think* you see, and not necessarily what's actually there. Pop always tells me it works pretty much the same way in real life.

On our way back from Rexleigh, Bo and I swung

by the hospital to see Mr. Lindstrom. I'd been over a number of times that week, but he was always sleeping. Pop told me they were keeping him pretty well drugged up, and I wondered if it might not be for their benefit as well as his.

It took us a few minutes to find the right room. First he'd been in intensive care, and then he'd gone into some kind of an open ward where if you wanted any privacy your only option was to pull a curtain around your bed. Knowing how Mr. Lindstrom felt about people in general, not to mention the fact that he couldn't sit up to pull the curtains if he wanted to, Pop had arranged for him to have a private room as soon as one opened up. I didn't know if Mr. Lindstrom had any insurance or if he could afford a private room, but I knew none of that would make any difference to Pop. He'd take care of it.

Mr. Lindstrom looked so pale and fragile lying there that, for a second, I thought we'd landed in the wrong room. I couldn't get used to seeing him when he wasn't in his overalls and an old cap. We walked over closer to the bed. I was pretty sure he recognized us. His eyes seemed to come to life somehow and he tried frantically to sit up. He got so agitated that at first I was afraid he'd have another stroke. I hurried over and sat in a chair near the head of the bed and put my hand on his shoulder.

"Don't try to get up," I said. "Bo and I just came by to see how you're doing." He relaxed somewhat back onto his pillow, but his eyes still had an urgent look to them. His hair was thinner than I remembered it being, and his face was somehow different. He was moving his mouth, and it took me a minute to realize the difference was that half his face was paralyzed; it just sat there like a mask. If anything, this had the effect of making the other half of his face seem even more animated.

"Ayn-yee," he said, struggling to get whatever it was he was trying to say out. "Ayn-yee."

I studied him as he tried to form words. At first I thought I'd been mistaken, that maybe he didn't know who I was and he was just spouting gibberish. But there was something about the intensity of how he was trying to speak that made me think again. When he drew a blank with me, his eyes traveled over to Bo.

"Ayn-yee," he kept saying, really pouring himself into the effort. "Ayn-yee." His eyes swung back to me and he reached for my hand and squeezed it. He didn't seem to have much strength even with his good hand.

I glanced over at Bo and could tell by the look on his face that he didn't have a clue either.

"I've got an idea," Bo said. He got off his chair and came up near me at the head of the bed. "Do you think you can write it?" he said to Mr. Lindstrom.

At this, Mr. Lindstrom squeezed harder on my hand. "Umm," he said, nodding as much as he was able to. "Ummmm."

Bo had already reached into his shirt pocket and pulled out the notepad he always carried to jot down ideas for filming or notes about things we'd discussed. A million times I'd told myself I should do the same thing, but the idea hadn't caught hold with me yet. It struck me as funny. *I* was the writer, and *Bo* carried the notepad around.

Bo crouched down by the bed. The first couple of times he placed his pen in Mr. Lindstrom's hand, it dropped onto the mattress, but on the third try he got a good grip on it. Then Bo held the notepad down in front of his hand. The whole thing felt like it took forever and seemed to call for everything Mr. Lindstrom had. His breathing became harder, and beads of sweat were standing out on his forehead. I leaned over the mattress, but from that angle I couldn't make out what he'd written.

Finally, Mr. Lindstrom dropped the pen and slumped back on his pillow. Bo turned the notepad around in front of us and both our heads leaned in to study it, almost doing one of those Three Stooges deals where their heads clunk together. It wasn't the most legible writing in the world, but there was no mistaking what it said.

"Andy," I said out loud, and when I did Mr. Lindstrom got excited again and found my hand and gave it another squeeze. "Ayn-yee," he managed to say one more time.

Bo and I looked at each other. And I could tell right away that the name on the pad didn't ring a bell with him any more than it did with me.

Late that night I finally made it over to check on Mr. Lindstrom's house. I don't know if I'd actually planned on going inside or if I was just going to check it out from the front, but when I got there I realized there was no way I was going in alone. Ethan and Pop had gone to dinner and then over to the hospital, and Bo and Rosasharn and even Jeremy (he'd finally managed to talk to the right Amy) all had dates and had left earlier to see a movie in Saratoga. They asked me to go with them, but I wasn't crazy about being the odd man out. I'd tried Katie one more time and missed her again, and I still hadn't left a message, I don't know—maybe I was afraid that if she knew I was calling her, she'd have an excuse all prepared why we couldn't go out—especially if it were true that her best friend had the hots for me.

Except for wishing I could be with Katie I didn't mind being on my own for a while. Earlier in the evening Bo and Rosasharn and Jeremy and I had set up at Blood Red Pond to shoot a couple of simple filler scenes. As soon as we took a break to eat, I took the offensive with Jeremy, trying to knock him off balance before he had the chance to do the same to me.

"Brie?" I said, holding it out in front of him. Brie was exactly the kind of thing guaranteed to make Jeremy crazy. I wasn't crazy about it myself. It was too strong, too much like something gone bad. But I'd made sure I had some in the cooler when I'd packed it up for the evening.

"Yuppie chow." Jeremy slapped my hand out from under his nose. "Mice won't even eat that stuff."

I opened the package so it could breathe and stuck it back under his nose.

Jeremy slapped my hand away again, harder this time, and got up and took his plate of food to the other side of the fire. I considered this a victory of sorts, but Jeremy hadn't thrown in the towel yet. He'd just retrenched.

He poked Rosasharn. "You know how Gabe-boy always thinks he's so smart. Well, I was reading some teacher magazine at Bo's that said they gave a math test to kids all around the world and the Irish scored second from the bottom."

"That's the *civilized* world, Jeremy," I told him. "*Your* people didn't even get to take it." Actually it would have been hard to say exactly who Jeremy's people were. His ancestors came from all over Europe, and he even had a little American Indian in him. I used to get him going by calling him the human mutt. Then, it seems, someone told him about the dangers of inbreeding, and he started feeling more secure in his diversity.

"How's your sister-uncle-cousin?" he said, getting in a lick about my pure Irish bloodline.

Rosasharn smacked him. "I can't believe you'd bring her up now. Didn't you hear? She died yesterday."

Jeremy smacked him back. "Shut up, ya tub."

And so it went on like that. And the funny thing is, Bo, who never argues with, insults, or mocks anybody, gets a bigger kick out of this than any of us. I swear he does. He always sits there with a little smile on his face taking it all in. Sometimes I even have the feeling we're staging these rank-athons just for his benefit.

Anyway, after the others left to get ready for their dates and pick up the girls, I stayed there reading by the fire. I'd probably been reading a good two or three hours and was almost to the end of my Emerson book when I got the idea to check on Mr. Lindstrom's house. It was time for me to head home for bed anyway, so I put out the fire, packed up what little stuff I had with me, and started out to the road.

Ordinarily, to get to Mr. Lindstrom's house from the pond, I would have taken the lane through the woods. Not only was it shorter, but I liked the soft feel of the grass and dead leaves and pine needles under my feet, and I loved walking under the big old trees that canopied the lane, at times so thickly you felt like you were walking through a tunnel. But that night I decided to take the long way around. Looking back on it, I remember noticing how pitch dark it had been and how quiet—you know, the kind of quiet where in the movies some guy always says it's *too* quiet. Also, I remember that as I was sitting by the fire, I looked up from my book a couple of times and had the strange sensation that I was being watched. Maybe I'm only remembering these things because of what I saw afterward and what I've since found out, but I don't think so. Feeling any kind of uneasiness about being in those woods was unusual for me. After all, I grew up thinking of these woods as my own backyard. Maybe the whole idea of being watched had been planted in my head by Ethan's new habit of staring out into the woods, or maybe it's like Bo always says, that everything in the universe is connected, and because of this I knew something was up before I even *knew* I knew something was up.

Anyway, the creepy feeling I'd developed while sitting around the campfire stayed with me even after I was out of the woods. When I walked by the spot where Walter Owens had found Mr. Lindstrom, I felt a chill go up my spine. All I could think of was what it must have been like for him lying out there all night, not completely unconscious, but probably not all there either, so it must have been like being stuck in some kind of nightmare—one where you're not even sure where you are or what's happening and all you know for sure is that you can't move. I hurried past and tried not to think about it. That's why, when I finally found myself in Mr. Lindstrom's yard looking up at his house, it took me so much by surprise.

At first I thought the light in the upstairs room was off. A closer look revealed that it wasn't, but the shade had been drawn, allowing only a sliver of light on either side.

I took a step back, and then another. A minute later I was out of the yard and on the road.

Thirteen

I started for home at a quick walk, but before I knew it I was jogging. Then, when I reached the stretch of road in front of Mr. Lindstrom's old barn, I all of a sudden remembered the thing Ray McPherson claimed to have seen scooting across the road there, and cranked it up another notch. I felt foolish, but I hit my lawn at a full run.

After I landed on the porch and had the security of the porch light overhead, I started feeling a little more rational again. First, I decided, I'd ask Pop if he'd been over to Mr. Lindstrom's taking care of things, or if maybe he'd finally heard from Mr. Lindstrom's daughter and *she'd* been around. And if we didn't come up with a logical explanation, we could go over and check on the house together. Things don't seem nearly as ominous when you're with somebody else, and that's especially true when that somebody is Pop.

Our house was quiet and, except for the center hallway, dark when I stepped inside. At first I thought both Pop and Ethan were already in bed. Then I heard the creak of Pop's chair in his study. I figured he hadn't heard me come through the door or else he would have run out to greet me. Generally whenever one of us steps through the door, it's a real homecoming for Pop.

I walked over to the study to say hello, but before I got there a familiar piano melody wafted out, and then I heard Shane MacGowan's voice. I sighed. Pop was holed up, listening to the Pogues again.

I'd bought Pop that Pogues CD a few Christmases ago. Pop's tough to shop for, but one thing you could always count on was Irish music—the good stuff, though, not the kind of grandmother stuff most people think of when you mention Irish music. Bo and I had gone to Celtic Treasures in Saratoga that year and the guy had said that if Pop was really true-blue Irish, he couldn't help but love the Pogues. He grabbed the disc and offered to play it for me, but I'd had such good luck with the Liam O'Flynn CD he'd recommended for Pop's birthday I bought the thing without listening to it. Afterward, I wasn't sure if I'd done the right thing.

The best song on the CD is called "Fairytale of New York," and when Pop heard it for the first time that Christmas, it actually brought tears to his eyes. I can't describe it exactly, but in some way it was as if he was seeing his own life in that song. It had hard drinking, a touch of sentimentality, and it most definitely had Pop's sense of humor. It had one more thing that always got to Pop: the story of a perfect love that had somehow taken a turn for the worse. The whole thing was Pop to a T. Not only that, but Shane MacGowan, the lead singer, even *sounded* just like Pop, having the same raspy, wistful voice that had always been Pop's trademark. Anyway, from that day on, whenever Pop would fall into a certain mood, he'd go into his study, plug in that Pogues CD, and play that song over and over.

The thing is, the song was so tragic and so hopeful at the same time that I could never be sure if it was pulling Pop up or dragging him down.

I waited in the hallway until after the song was over and Pop had clicked it off with the remote. Then I stepped into the doorway, but didn't say anything right away. There was an eerie stillness to the room that made me think of a wax museum for some reason. Pop sat frozen in his rocking chair, not rocking or puffing on his pipe, or even rubbing his temples the way he sometimes did after a long day. The room was dark, but I could see his outline clearly enough, backlit from the light of the stereo.

"Hi, Pop," I said, kind of softly, wondering if maybe he'd started to fall asleep in his chair.

The chair turned slightly in my direction. "Gabriel?" Pop said hoarsely and almost as if it were a question. "I didn't hear you come in."

"How're you doing, Pop?" I walked into the room and sat in the chair opposite him.

"I'm not making any serious plans to check out quite yet," Pop said, but you wouldn't have known it from the tone of his voice. He tried to laugh and couldn't even pull that off.

"How's Mr. Lindstrom?" I had kind of a sinking feeling about this. The way Pop was acting made me think the worst had happened.

"Hanging in there," Pop said, nodding. "Hanging in there as well as can be expected."

"That's good," I said. "He seemed to be looking a little better when Bo and I saw him this morning. Maybe he'll be able to come home soon."

"God willing," Pop said, and nodded thoughtfully. "God willing."

I waited to see if he'd say anything more. He studied me a minute before going on.

"Gabriel, there's something I should tell you. I was hoping I wouldn't have to, but now I think it's time I did."

I felt my stomach tighten. Announcing that he had something to say just wasn't Pop's style and didn't seem like a good omen.

"She's hit him with a lawsuit," he said. He was looking out the window, but it was too dark out there to see anything.

"A lawsuit?" I said, puzzled and relieved at the same time. "Who?" Pop wasn't always the most linear of thinkers, and I was used to having to guess which direction he was coming in from. He'd often agonize over different cases he was working on, and I thought at first maybe he meant the girl with the dead cat was suing her ex-boyfriend.

"The papers were served on him three or four weeks ago," Pop continued, still staring out the window. "I've no doubt the whole business contributed to the stroke. He came to me right away, upset, of course . . . more upset than I'd ever seen him—angry, embarrassed, hurt, confused, all rolled into one. I got hold of her lawyer and tried to set up a meeting between her and her father, but she refused. She didn't want to have anything to do with him, except through her lawyer." He gave kind of a helpless wave of his arms. "It's moot now," he said, "since John couldn't sit through a meeting anyway. But it's hard going there every day and seeing the same questions in his eyes: 'Did you hear from her?' 'Is she coming?' And each time I have to tell him no, I can see the hurt in those eyes. I'm sure he thought that whatever their differences had been, she'd want to see him now."

I took all this in. Of course, I knew now it was Mr. Lindstrom's daughter he was talking about—that she was suing him and wouldn't speak to him—but other than that none of it made much sense to me. "Why's she suing him?" I asked.

Pop turned and looked me in the eye. "Rachel—that's her name—is seeking punitive damages for prolonged physical abuse, claiming, among other things, that his violence toward her over the years has damaged her chances of ever having a healthy relationship with a man."

"Mr. *Lindstrom* abused his daughter?" I said, my jaw dropping down.

"Unfortunately, that very reaction is what makes cases of this sort so difficult. People hear the word *abuse* and automatically react with horror and indignation. It's not the kind of thing anybody wants to appear to condone, so it makes it that much harder to get a client a fair shake."

"Do you think he did it?"

Pop gave a little shrug. "It's not just a matter of 'did it' or 'didn't do it.' John was never one to spare the rod, as they used to say. He doesn't deny that. He had two good hands and a leather strap, and he used them when he saw fit—probably generously, if I know John."

I wondered what Pop thought of this. He'd never in his life raised a hand against either Ethan or me. He never needed to. For one thing he was so easygoing it was rare for him to get upset enough, at least with us, to even *want* to. For another thing, when he asked us to do something, and told us he really wanted us to do it, we went and did it—simple as that. Even if it meant apologizing to somebody like Mrs. Quinby, which I wouldn't have done in a million years on my own.

"Do you think he's guilty?" I said, trying my question a different way.

Pop shrugged again. "The question *is*—guilty of what? Of losing his temper? Of striking someone? Of raising his kids the way he was raised, and the way I was raised?" He ran a hand through his gray hair, which late at night tended to be even wilder than usual, giving him a kind of Mark-Twain-Meets-Einstein look. "It's a funny time we're living through, Gabriel. I've lived for a while, maybe too long, but I've never seen a time when so many people were blaming each other for so many things. You read the papers. . . . You watch TV. It's almost all you see. Every day my young client from that cat-poisoning affair gets treated to an earful of invectives from the animal lovers who line up outside before he's escorted into the courtroom. If you could see their faces, contorted with a raw and ugly hatred. . . . And the things they shout . . . some of their suggested punishments . . . I'd be embarrassed to tell you. They have no way of knowing for certain if he's even *guilty,* and there's at least some evidence to suggest he's not. Even if he is, shouldn't he be included as one of the creatures covered by this outpouring of love they insist motivates their interest in the whole affair?" He leaned back in his chair and took a deep breath. "I sometimes wonder whether, if Jesus were to reappear now, he'd dare try that 'Let he who is without sin cast the first stone' business again. If he did, I suspect prudent men everywhere would duck for cover from the onslaught of the 'pure at heart.'" He reached over for his pipe and held it, but didn't light it. "The truth is we all come into the world imperfect, and whether we like to admit it or not, we've all caused our share of harm to others, through stubbornness, or self-ishness, or just plain weakness. And maybe because I've caused *more* than my share, it disturbs me to see just how unforgiving people can be. I don't know—maybe I'm afraid this is all a preview of my own Judgment Day."

I thought about this. The idea of Judgment Day had always fascinated me. I'd read a couple of different books by people who claimed to have died and come back to life, and they both said the same thing—that Judgment Day actually consists of *you* judging yourself. You sit there and watch your life play out before you, and you see not only all the things you've done, but how those things have affected others. Supposedly the pain that comes from this can be excruciating, because you see your actions with total clarity, stripped of all the rationalizations you'd wrapped them up in during your life. I couldn't help but think that if this were true, maybe Pop was getting a head start on the rest of us. He'd always been hard on himself.

"You're a good person, Pop," I said. "The best I know."

Pop smiled sadly. "That generous statement is undoubtedly more of a testament to your goodness than mine, Gabriel. But right now I should be more concerned with John than the state of my own pitiful soul. This whole business has already taken quite a toll on him. As I say, it probably helped bring on his stroke, and I'm afraid it's affecting his mind as well. I finally realized today what he's been trying to tell me all week. He actually thinks he saw his son on the night of his stroke."

"The guy who was killed in the car accident?"

Pop nodded. "I wish you could have known him. He was as kind and sweet and gentle as anyone you could ever meet. And *talented?* He could fix anything on wheels. Oh, how he loved cars—the faster, the better. It couldn't be fast enough to suit him. He'd take an old junk heap and fiddle with it till that thing could practically fly." Pop finally lit his pipe, puffed on it a few times, and sat there in a cloud of smoke, remembering. "Ironically, it was his love of fast cars that turned out to be his undoing. That was an awful night, that was. I'll never forget it. And even though the years have come and gone, John never really got over Andy's death."

I sat up straighter. So that's who Andy was. Andy *Lindstrom*. He was the boy in the picture I'd been studying the day we cleaned Mr. Lindstrom's house.

Pop had enough on his mind, but I had a question that just couldn't wait any longer. "Pop," I said, "were you over at Mr. Lindstrom's house within the last few days?"

Pop nodded. "Today. I had to pick up a few papers. Why?"

"Did you go upstairs?

He shook his head. "I'm afraid I didn't make it that far. I told John what a splendid cleaning job you did on the downstairs though. Don't tell me you're tackling the upstairs now too."

I shook my head. "It'd be nice, though—for when he comes home."

"It would indeed," Pop said. "It would indeed."

Actually I wasn't thinking much about cleaning at that moment. I was thinking how I'd be helping Jeremy stack some hay the next day, and how after we were done I'd talk him into going with me to see what the deal was at Mr. Lindstrom's house. We'd do it together, and we'd do it in the daylight. And I wouldn't have to worry Pop about the whole thing.

Fourteen

"How'd the date go?" I asked Jeremy before I even got off my bike. "I hear Amy's mom is very nice."

"It was better than the date *you* had," Jeremy answered. I had to admit, he was getting better at this all the time.

The main haymow was already filled, and we started in on one of the old dilapidated barns off to the side. This particular barn had plenty of boards missing from its sides, not to mention an entire open section facing east, so it wasn't as stifling as it had been in the main haymow. It was hot enough, but nothing compared to before. Our main problem this time was entirely different. It seems that by setting up shop there, we were challenging the territorial rights of a group of not-so-hospitable bumblebees. I never did find out where their nest was located, but they'd fly in through the open east section, buzz around our heads a few times, and then fly out again. I'm not crazy about bees, but I've never had any major problems with them. Jeremy, on the other hand, had a long history of disputes with every kind of bee you could imagine. The trouble was, Jeremy couldn't just let a bee fly by. If there was one within swatting range, he seemed to feel it was his civic duty to swat at it. I don't think this was a decision on his part, but more like some kind of a spastic reflex. Whatever the reason, the bees did not appreciate the attention. Before we'd finished stacking the first load, Jeremy had been stung twice.

"Just *ignore* them," I advised after the first time.

"Shut up," he advised back, trying to twist around

to check on the welt that was forming on his back.

"Have it your way," I told him. "Just make sure you let them know I'm not with you."

"Shut up."

By the middle of the second load I was pretty much on my own as far as stacking hay went. Jeremy's skirmishes with the bees had escalated to an all-out war, and he was losing ground fast. At one point, while he was swatting at the enemy in front of him, a battalion circled behind him and started dive-bombing on his bare back. Before I knew it, Jeremy was doing some diving of his own—off the hay we'd (I'd) stacked and down onto the dirt floor. He rolled to his feet and shot out the door, with the bees in hot pursuit. It was one of the funniest things I'd ever seen, and I had to sit down, I was laughing so hard. I didn't get to stay seated long though. With Jeremy gone, a few of the leftover bees fixed their attention on me, proving—since *I* hadn't done anything to them—that even bees can be bigots, and I ended up diving in the dirt and retreating the same way Jeremy had.

Even as I was galloping across the yard, I could hear Jeremy's father's happy guffaws from the wagon. He was still chuckling five minutes later when Jeremy and I returned, our backs covered in dabs of aloe vera lotion his mother had supplied.

"You boys ready to go back to work?" he said as we flopped to the ground in front of the wagon.

Jeremy looked up at him as if he'd lost his mind. "There's bees in there," he said, pointing angrily at the old barn.

"You're gonna let a few bees call the shots?" Mr. Wulfson said, pretending to be totally perplexed at such a state of affairs. He motioned for us to follow him.

Jeremy and I looked at each other and shrugged. We

then followed him into the barn, the two of us practically tiptoeing, and keeping a sharp eye out for bees. Mr. Wulfson stopped just inside the barn and turned back toward the opening. He had his hand on the brim of his hat as if he were about to tip it to a lady, but of course that wasn't what he had in mind. The first bumblebee that sailed through the opening was snapped out of the air with a flick of his wrist. The bee fell to the dirt, and the cap returned to Mr. Wulfson's head. He repeated this simple motion many more times in the next few minutes, laughing after each swat and seeming to get a big kick out of the whole thing. Jeremy and I watched in awe as a little pile of bees started forming around his feet.

"We can't be lettin' a few bees dictate policy, now, can we, boys?" he said happily. "Here, Jem"—that's what he called Jeremy—"you keep this cap on your head and if one of those fellas gets too close, you snap him into a better world." He flicked the hat once more to demonstrate.

Jeremy scowled at the cap for a few seconds and then put it on his head. Mr. Wulfson returned to the wagon, turned on the elevator, and started loading hay onto it again. A few minutes later I became aware of a commotion going on behind me and turned to see what it was. Jeremy had his father's hat in his hand and was going A-1 nutso, dancing around like somebody possessed and swatting in every direction for all he was worth. I couldn't even see any bees, but that may have been because I was laughing too hard. Two minutes later we both dove out of there and onto the dirt again.

• • •

After lunch Jeremy and I got on our bikes and headed out to Mr. Lindstrom's house. Jeremy was still in kind of a foul mood, even though I'd been extremely nice to him, courteously thanking him a number of times for the free entertainment, and forgiving him for the welts on my back, which, I was quick to explain, were all his fault and still hurt more than you might think—aloe vera lotion or not.

"Ooouuuu, I'm so scared," Jeremy mocked after we'd dropped our bikes in the yard and he caught me staring up at the house. "There's a ghost in there that pulls shades down. Ooouuu."

"Too bad you didn't bring your father's hat with you," I said. "Then you could swat it."

"Shut up," he told me.

We climbed onto the porch. As I stuck my key in the door, I started feeling a little silly about how I'd bolted away from there the night before. The place didn't seem nearly so creepy now. Of course, it's hard to work up too much fear when you have somebody like Jeremy right on your heels going "Oooouuuu, I'm so scared" every two minutes.

I took a quick peek into the living room, which still looked pretty good, except for a little film of dust that had already started to settle over everything, and then headed for the staircase. I stopped at the top and thought for a second, trying to decide which room I'd seen the light in. Jeremy made another ghost noise.

"You know, Jeremy, you actually make a better ghost than you do a person."

"Shut up," he said in his person voice.

There was only one door open in the upstairs hallway, and it was on the wrong side of the house. Any windows from that room would face the backyard, not the front. Still, since that was the door that was open, we walked over to take a look.

Even from the doorway it was obvious that this was

Mr. Lindstrom's room. To say it had a lived-in look would be a gross understatement. The whole room was like an industrial-sized hamper. Dirty clothes were strewn everywhere, the bed gave new meaning to the word "unmade," and the smell was . . . well . . . almost as bad as it had been in the kitchen. We didn't bother going in to investigate any further.

"Let's find the room that had the light on," I said.

"Let's find a room that doesn't stink," Jeremy added.

We headed across the hall. It felt strange being up there, and I still had the feeling that we were violating privacy—not just Mr. Lindstrom's but the whole family's, even though they were all long gone.

"This could be the one," I said with my hand on the knob to the first door right of the staircase.

"Then open it, scrub."

I did. Right away I knew it was a girl's room, so it must have been Rachel's, the daughter who'd left home and was now suing her father. Except for the dust and cobwebs, it was actually cleaner than Mr. Lindstrom's. There were still some things on the walls—a picture of John Travolta dancing in *Saturday Night Fever*, another picture of the Bee Gees, and next to that, a picture of the *Mod Squad*, which couldn't have looked more *un*-mod if it'd been Julius Caesar and the gang.

"You could get polyester poisoning in here," I said.

"Huh?" Jeremy gave me his what-are-you-babbling-about look.

"The pictures," I explained. "All the guys in the pictures are wearing polyester."

"What do you care?" Jeremy said.

I walked into the room, starting to get into the whole idea of snooping. All around the bed and in front of the desk were posters of beautiful scenes from nature—really obvious things like sunsets and mountain streams—each one ruined by having a corny message plastered across it about love and peace and happiness. There was one poster of a butterfly that said something about love being like a butterfly—hold on to it too hard and it'll die, but let it go and it'll return to you on its own.

Jeremy walked over and scowled at that one. "If you let it go, why wouldn't it just fly away for good?" he said in that rational way of his that never failed to crack me up.

"Maybe you're only supposed to do it with a trained butterfly," I told him.

Jeremy didn't say anything but his look said "shut up" for him. As he wandered back into the hall, he was still shaking his head—maybe about the poster or maybe about my trained-butterfly joke. I started out after him and then, remembering what I was doing there, checked the shade on the window (which was up) and the lights (which were off).

The next room down the hall was definitely a boy's room. It had to be Andy's. There were pictures of hopped-up Camaros and Mustangs as well as a few Ferraris and Lamborghinis hanging on the walls. It seemed kind of funny—the kid who Pop said was sweet and gentle had things like race cars on his walls, and the one who was suing her own father and wouldn't even visit him after his stroke had posters about love and peace on hers. Or maybe not so funny; maybe the idea is you hang up things that you *wish* you had.

Anyway, the predominant theme in Andy's room was definitely cars, and on one dresser there were a few pictures of him standing next to different cars he'd prob-ably owned—the first a Mustang, a seventy-something one, which is when they were seriously ugly, and the next a Camaro that didn't look half bad. Both of them had wide tires in the back with skinnier ones in front and both had jacked-up rear ends. On his desk, in an eight-by-ten frame, was the school picture I'd seen downstairs and figured was his senior picture. He was looking out on the world with a shy smile, and I thought again that it was probably not long after this was taken that he was killed. Above the desk, tacked onto a bulletin board, was another picture that caught my eye. It was of a kid in a pair of cutoffs standing in front of some kind of river or lake. I pulled the picture down and looked at it closer. I knew it was Andy even before I read the back, which said "Andy at Rexleigh Bridge" in handwriting that was probably his mother's. I turned the picture over and studied it some more. You couldn't see the bridge, but behind the kid you could see people splashing around in the water and then some tree branches hanging down off to the side.

The thing that caught my attention, though, was the kid himself, Andy, squinting into the sun and grinning in that kid kind of way where you couldn't be sure if he was smiling or smirking, but you couldn't help but smile back at him. With a few scattered freckles and the sandy-colored hair hanging down over his eyes—eyes that seemed to be smiling along with the rest of him—he could have been cast as Tom Sawyer. I looked back to the school picture and saw that it was just an older version of the same face. He was one of those kids who'd made the transition from kid to young man without any major facial traumas, having almost the same delicate features at eighteen that he'd had at twelve. This was undoubtedly thanks to his mother, who had the same kind of features herself.

Jeremy had opened the closet door, and I could hear him scrounging around in there. When he came out he was holding a shotgun.

"Anybody you wanna shoot?" he said.

"You have to ask?" I told him.

Jeremy went back inside and scrounged around some more. I set the snapshot in my hand next to the other picture of Andy on the desk and started checking the lights in the room. All off. Then I walked over to the window. The shade was up. I stood there and looked down the driveway to where I had been standing the night before.

"This is so strange," I said.

"What?" Jeremy said from the closet.

"The whole thing's bizarre. I *know* I saw a light in one of these rooms, and I *know* the shade was down." Suddenly another thought hit me—something I'd seen, but it just hadn't registered. "Jeremy, come 'ere."

He took his sweet time about it, but he came out holding an old car magazine. "What now, scrub?"

"You notice anything different about this room from the last one we checked?"

"Better posters," he said.

"No," I said. "*Cobwebs.* There's no cobwebs. And look. . . ." I swiped a finger across a dresser in the corner. "No dust. It's like it's just been cleaned. Even the downstairs has dust, and we just did that last week."

"Oooouuu," Jeremy said, tossing the magazine on the bed, "a ghost that cleans." But even he seemed to be wondering a little bit. Myself, I was beginning to have a strange feeling about that room—as if . . . I don't know . . . as if it contained some kind of a *presence,* for lack of a better word. And I couldn't help remembering what Mr. Lindstrom had said about seeing Andy.

I went back to the desk and looked at the two pictures of Andy again. Both of them smiled up at me.

Fifteen

Later that afternoon we all met to do another shoot at Blood Red Pond. Even though Green Guy and his family were pretty much creatures of the night, my script called for the whole clan to go into family counseling, and since their counselor was human, they had to adjust their schedules accordingly. I took some razzing from everybody for managing to drag a Mrs. Quinby type into even a swamp monster flick, of course. Jeremy shook his head and said again, "The kid's obsessed," and Bo followed with, "Yeah, but at least with Gabe there's no guessing. You always know a psychologist stands for a psychologist."

Bo had gotten off work at four, and we were all set up to begin when he arrived. I'd gone home after snooping around Mr. Lindstrom's place with Jeremy, figuring I'd check in on Ethan and maybe help him with Cappy for a while if he wanted. Ethan's bike was home but he was nowhere to be found. I knew he hadn't ridden into town with Pop because Pop had left for Albany on business in the morning, so I figured maybe he'd gone for a walk or something on his own. It seemed like Ethan was doing a lot more on his own lately, and I felt a little bad about that. Part of it may have been just that he was getting older, but I was afraid at least some of it might have been that I was always so busy with my thoughts and activities that I left him hanging too much on his own and maybe he'd decided he wasn't waiting for me anymore. A few times in the last few days when I'd come across him, he'd looked up at me kind of surprised, as if he had a secret he wasn't sharing. Part of me figured it was good that he was becoming more independent, but a bigger part of me missed having him waiting around for me so we could do things together.

I took a shower, and when I went to get dressed I had another surprise. Now my backup pair of jeans was missing. And while I was pawing around for them, I discovered my green pocket tee was gone too. Then, when I went down to the laundry room to drop off my sweaty working-on-the-farm clothes and to see if there was any folded clean stuff available, what do I spot but my missing Key West henley on top of the dirty-laundry pile. And right under them were my original missing jeans. This was very strange. Jennie must've done four wash loads since they'd disappeared, not to mention that I could've sworn they'd been in a *clean*-clothes pile the last I'd seen them. This kind of thing had always been pretty much the story of my life, but now it was getting out of hand. I trudged back up to my room and dug out some backup things to my backup things.

Ethan showed up about twenty minutes before we were supposed to meet at the pond. I was loading up the cooler, because we planned on staying there right through dinner. I wasn't having much more luck with the food than I'd had with the clothes.

"Hey, Ethan," I said as he pulled some Wheat Thins out of the cupboard and set them by the cooler, "didn't Pop just bring home a bunch of Cajun shrimp yesterday? And some seafood salad?"

Ethan kind of shrugged and went back to the cupboard. I waited for him to say something, but he didn't.

"Where'd all that stuff go?" I said.

Ethan plunked some nachos down next to the Wheat Thins. "I ate it," he said, looking up at me apologetically.

"You ate it *all?*" Ethan can hold his own when it comes to eating, but he's still fairly pint-sized and he doesn't even like Cajun shrimp that much.

"Sorry," he said, and he looked it too.

"No," I said, thinking I'd come on too strong. "You can eat whatever you want." I reached back into the refrigerator and pulled out some deli turkey. "We've still got plenty of stuff." I grabbed some lettuce and mayonnaise and a loaf of bread. "Come on. We'd better take off or they'll be waiting."

A half hour later the Green family was all suited up and I was giving them the once-over before Bo arrived.

"Nothing personal," I told them, "but you guys look like doo-doo in the daylight." I said it kind of without thinking, or maybe thinking Jeremy would be the only one who'd take offense, and was kind of surprised when I saw Sudie giving me a look. Then it hit me that she was the one who made their costumes. "Of course, I don't mean 'doo-doo' in a bad way," I explained with a lame smile.

"Yeah, right," she said, looking over the rims of her glasses at me. Sudie didn't actually wear glasses, but she was going to be playing our counselor, and we were following the time-honored film and TV convention of making someone look intellectual by sticking a pair of glasses on her face. It didn't work any better now than it ever did, but that didn't matter. We were playing the scene for laughs anyway.

I'd ordered some counselor props from a company in New Jersey that specialized in selling every kind of baloney that ever came down the pike to help people "heal." I got "The Feelings Game" (which turned out to be the same one we'd used with Mrs. Quinby) for Green Guy and Green Gal to play, and since Ethan was too shy to speak on camera, I decided on a "feelings" wall chart for him. It had all these different clown faces on it in pockets all around a Ferris wheel, and as the catalog put it, "When the child wants to express a certain feeling, he takes the clown face from the pocket and places it in the center of the wheel (it stays on by the magic of Velcro!)." When I called the 1-800 number and tried to place the order, the lady on the other end asked me if I was a licensed therapist. Being caught a little off-guard I said no, and she almost wouldn't send me the stuff. Finally she checked with some higher-up, and after a few minutes' discussion they must have decided it was all right. What did they think—that the sad-faced clown in the wrong hands might cause serious damage to a kid? Those people kill me.

Filming the scene was almost easier than ordering the props. Sudie was really becoming a decent actress, not to mention a complete ham when she wanted to be, but she played it completely straight, guiding this goofy family through their goofy therapy. Each time Ethan put a clown face expressing what he was supposedly feeling in the center of the Ferris wheel, she made a big deal out of it just like Mrs. Quinby would have, explaining in an unscripted aside to the camera how important it is to "affirm children's feelings whenever appropriate." Ethan was hamming it up too. By the end of the scene, he was flinging those feelings up there one after the other, and Sudie could hardly keep up with all the affirming she owed him. Meanwhile, Green Guy and Green Gal were busy describing off-the-wall scenarios about when they felt each of the feelings they'd landed on in "The Feelings Game." In a little over an hour we had more than enough usable footage, as well as pains in our sides from laughing so hard.

Even with all that was going on, I couldn't help but notice that every so often Ethan would look out into the woods as if he'd seen something or was *expecting* to see something. I asked him once what he was looking for, and he just shrugged and right away went back to reading his script. I may be a little dense about a lot of things, but I was slowly getting the idea that he knew more than he was letting on about some of the stuff that had been happening around these parts—my missing clothes, the food shortages, and maybe even the strange sightings by Ray McPherson and Mr. Lindstrom. I took a long look into the area of the woods where I'd caught Ethan sneaking peeks, but of course I didn't see anything. Sighing, I decided all I could do was keep my eyes open and wait until whatever was going on became obvious enough that even I couldn't miss it.

That evening, as we sat around the fire, Rosasharn reached over and grabbed Jeremy, saying he had a feeling he wanted to share. Jeremy proceeded to share what *he* was feeling. He smacked Rosasharn on the side of the head.

"I think I should order Jeremy a self-esteem coloring book," I said.

"Shut up," he said.

We laughed at the idea of scowly-faced Jeremy with crayons and then gradually drifted off into our own thoughts. Jeremy got up and started stoking the fire.

"You wanna know what gets me?" he said, and

threw on a couple of big sticks. He actually waited until we all nodded our heads. "Campaign posters," he then announced.

"*Campaign* posters?" I said. The thing was it was June and nobody'd seen any campaign posters in months.

"Yeah," he said. "They're so stupid. You see this poster sitting on somebody's lawn or someplace, and the thing says maybe three words, like 'Vote for Hincky' or something like that, and it doesn't even tell you anything *about* the guy. So what's supposed to happen? A week later you're in the voting booth ready to vote for the other guy and all of a sudden you think, 'Hey, wait. That poster said to vote for Hincky.' It's so stupid. Who's gonna change their vote because of an idiotic poster that doesn't even tell you anything?"

"I don't know about you," Rosasharn said, "but Hincky's got my vote."

Jeremy was so wrapped up in what he was saying he didn't even call Rosasharn a tub or tell him to shut up. "You know what else is stupid?" he said. "Those bumper stickers that say SCHOOL'S OUT. DRIVE CAREFULLY. If they're gonna have those, then how come they don't have some that say SCHOOL'S BACK IN SESSION. DRIVE CRAZY AGAIN."

You could see he was getting all wound up and was developing a kind of momentum. His face was all earnest and intense, as if these things were more important than peace in the Middle East. More than once Bo has told me that I look the same way when I get up on my high horse. Still, that didn't stop me from getting a charge out of Jeremy's performance. Everybody else seemed to be enjoying it too.

"And you know those BABY ON BOARD stickers?"

Jeremy continued. "Like your car is going out of control and you're about to crash into somebody, but all of a sudden you see that sticker and decide ya better hit somebody else. Gimme a break."

Jeremy was working the fire harder now, sending up a shower of sparks every time he poked at it. Meanwhile he went on listing everything he could think of that rubbed him the wrong way, till all of us, including Ethan, were just about rolling in the dirt. Finally he noticed the reaction he was getting and offered his standard advice.

"Shut up," he told us.

Bo stayed at my house that night. He would have just as soon we stayed out at the pond, but I nixed the idea. The one camp-out we'd already had had pretty much cured me of that for the season. Bo and I had stayed at each other's houses so much over the years that we both had our own beds in both places. When we were little kids, we probably could have disappeared from the face of the earth, and for a few days everybody would have just thought we were at the other one's house.

After we'd undressed and climbed into bed, I suddenly remembered something I'd been wanting to talk with him about.

"Did you know Mr. Lindstrom had a daughter?" I asked him.

He shrugged. "I saw some pictures at his house and I guess I figured one of them was his daughter. Why?"

"I found out last night she's suing him." I knew none of this was *legally* confidential, but it seemed personal enough that I wouldn't have told anybody about it except Bo.

Bo leaned up on one elbow and looked at me. "Why?" He sounded the same way I did when Pop told me.

I sat up. "She says he used to hit her, and now it's his fault she has trouble getting along with guys."

Neither of us said anything for a minute. I was thinking about how it was that you could hate your own father so much you wouldn't even want to see him when he was in the hospital—maybe dying. Then I remembered reading one time about people actually going to the graves of their parents and performing some kind of homemade divorce ceremony—their way of washing their hands of them, giving them the final kiss-off. The whole thing made me feel terrible.

"It just doesn't seem right," I said. "I mean, genetically speaking you *are* your parents, right? So if you hate them. . . ."

Bo had sat up in his bed, Indian style. His hand went up and started playing with the red coral pendant he always wears on a gold chain. He'd worn it ever since he was a little kid. When he fiddled with it like that, it always meant he was thinking. "And it's karmic too," he said. "If you plant cabbages, it doesn't make sense to blame somebody else when you don't get carrots."

That's another one of the things I like about Bo. Every once in a while he'll come out with a statement that sounds like something the old blind guy on the old *Kung Fu* show would say.

I already knew a thing or two about the law of karma. That had been the subject of more than one of our all-night discussions over the years. Basically it says that everything that comes to you is the result of what you've sent out. Bo always told me it's kind of like receiving a package you've mailed to yourself. I thought about that for a minute. "So you're saying she had it coming?" I said. "That it was her own fault?"

Bo thought about that. "Maybe it's more like this. Say you're a runner and you strap on ankle weights because you know it'll make your legs stronger. And then as soon as you get out on the track, you forget you did it. You look around at everybody else running around *without* ankle weights and you start thinking how unfair it is. Why should *you* have to wear ankle weights when nobody else does? And then you start using up energy feeling sorry for yourself, and maybe even blaming other people for your predicament. And it's all because you don't remember you're the one who put the weights there in the first place."

"And if you *did* remember . . . ?"

Bo shrugged. "You wouldn't feel bad about them anymore," he said. "You'd start to see how they were making you stronger."

I have to admit this kind of thinking appealed to me—the idea of each person being in his own driver's seat. It was what I liked about Emerson and the whole "Self-Reliance" thing. It seemed like this could turn into one of our all-night discussions, so I figured I might as well get a glass of water. "You want some?" I asked Bo.

"With a twist," he said, and cocked an eyebrow.

"How about I twist your head," I said, giving him a jab on the way out.

As I padded down the hall toward the upstairs bathroom, I thought about Rachel some more. If Bo was right, then Rachel's real battle was with herself, not with her father. I wondered if that were true of all of us, if all our battles were really with ourselves.

I was coming out of the bathroom and lost in this

line of thought when I heard something from down-stairs. At first I thought maybe Pop was down there putting on the Pogues or something. But as I stood there listening, I could make out the faint sound of snoring coming from his room. I froze for a second, trying to decide if I should investigate on my own or go back and get Bo first. Then, figuring it was probably just Ethan, who had a habit of sneaking out late at night to check on Cappy, I set down the glasses and headed for the stairs, but tiptoeing, just in case. When I reached the bottom and rounded the corner, I saw some light coming from the kitchen. I crept forward, slower and more careful than ever. Before I was halfway there, I heard a little thunk and the kitchen went dark. From years of personal experience I recog-nized that thunk as our refrigerator door closing and it explained why the kitchen went dark as well. I picked up my pace a little.

Just before I reached the doorway to the kitchen I heard the back door close. Figuring that Ethan had grabbed a snack and left to visit Cappy, I flicked on the light, planning to scoot across the kitchen and go out to the barn with him. I hadn't gone even a step when I ran head-on into him.

We both almost had heart attacks on the spot.

Sixteen

Between almost having that heart attack in the kitchen and then staying up half the night discussing karma and dharma and reaping what you sow, it's not surprising that I woke up late and on the wrong side of the bed. Running might have helped but I didn't really feel like it, and Ethan already had Cappy out, which probably meant he'd given up on the idea too. I started the day feeling off balance—a little antsy, edgy, and thinking more than ever that *something* wasn't as it should be. One of the things that kept replaying in my head was how Ethan had acted when I ran into him. Not the way he'd jumped, which was understandable, but how he'd behaved afterward: not looking me in the eye, and acting like he was in a big hurry to get back to bed. Of course I probably came across as the Grand Inquisitor, wanting to know why I'd heard the back door close if he hadn't been going outside, *and* if he'd just raided the refrigerator why he wasn't carrying any food. I never did get any answers.

Bo had left early for the country club, and Pop—after serving up his usual Sunday brunch—had loaded Ethan into the car and headed for the hospital to check in on Mr. Lindstrom. I could have gone with them, or I could have gone and hung around the pro shop with Bo, but I thought at the time it might be nice to hang around the house alone. It wasn't.

I tried studying a little biology until I couldn't take it anymore, and then decided the lawn could use mowing and charged into that. After I'd bounced around the yard on our Cub Cadet for an hour and then spent another fifteen minutes trimming with the push mower, the whole yard was in tip-top shape and I was as antsy as ever. As I was putting the push mower back into the barn, I saw Ray McPherson roll by slowly in his old Buick. I waved and he waved back. Ray had been driving by more than usual, it seemed to me, since Rosasharn had done that deranged-seal act on the hood of his car. I figured he was hoping to catch a glimpse of what he probably thought was some kind of missing link running loose in these parts. That might have been funny if I hadn't been busy wondering what the deal was around here myself.

I went upstairs and took another shot at studying biology, which lasted all of about two minutes, and then tried reading my Emerson book, which lasted about fifteen. Next I took a walk over to the pond, hoping that being out in nature might help me to unwind a little. After sitting on an old log staring out across the water and fidgeting for a half hour or so, I continued on down the lane and circled around until I was standing in front of Mr. Lindstrom's house. I scanned the upstairs windows for a minute to see if everything looked the way it had been when I was there with Jeremy the day before. The shades were all up, and the house sat looking bleached-out and sad in the afternoon sun. It seemed like a place that had been deserted for months, not just days.

When my eyes came back to the ground, I noticed that Mr. Lindstrom's lawn was looking pretty sad and neglected too, being about three times more overgrown than ours had been, so I decided to take care of that while I was there. I went into the storage shed that was attached to the side of his house and found his old Toro mower—power, but one of the antique jobs with a roll of curved blades that turn over a stationary cutter bar. It was crude, but I'd seen it work, which it did pretty well, at least for clipping, although it didn't chop the grass at all so it wasn't great for mulching. Not that Mr. Lindstrom gave two hoots about that. I checked to make sure it had enough gas, then wrapped the old pull rope around whatever the thing you wrap it around is called and gave it a yank. It sputtered a few times but didn't really catch until I found the choke and flicked it closed. Then one more pull and it started up and ran like a charm.

It took me a few minutes to get the hang of the thing. The rotating blades and the wheels weren't geared separately, so there was no moving the wheels without the blades going too. That meant if you wanted to cross the driveway you had to raise the handle up high to get the cutter bar out of the dirt or you'd be firing rocks and dirt into your shins, not to mention the damage you'd be doing to the blades and cutter bar in the process. And when you went into heavy grass and it started to plug, you played it just the opposite, pushing down on the handle, which raised the drive wheels off the ground and gave things a chance to clear. Before I learned this I'd stalled it out a couple of times.

By the time I'd made a couple of swipes back and forth in front of the house I felt like an old pro, really booking through the lighter patches of grass and letting it feed more slowly where the grass turned to something more like hay.

As I was in the middle of a U-turn after my third or forth swipe, I took one of my many glances up at the house, and what I saw, or at least what I *thought* I saw, sent a jolt straight up my back. I could've sworn I'd seen a figure in an upstairs window. I hadn't seen it dead-on, so I wasn't left with any clear image of it in my mind. It was more of a *sense* of something being there as my eyes flicked over the side of the house; first it was there and then, as my eyes flicked back, it was gone. And to make things even eerier, the window in question was the one to Andy's room.

My first thought, if *fear* can be considered a thought, was that I should leave the mower right where it sat and make serious tracks out of there, and I almost did just that. But when I looked at the window again, sitting there so still and innocent in the middle of that desolate house, I began to question whether I'd actually seen anything in the first place. Imagination can be a funny thing—even while my heart was still racing, I knew it could have been nothing more than the way the afternoon light had hit the window as I was making the turn or some kind of reflection of the big box elder. Finally I convinced myself that the whole thing was just my imagination working overtime and decided to hold my ground. It may have been a matter of pride. It'd been one thing running home from that place like a scared rabbit at night—I didn't feel like doing the same thing in broad daylight. I kept mowing, but I felt good and creepy all while I was doing it, and with the noise of the mower making it impossible to hear if anybody was approaching me, every second I was half expecting something to come up and tap me on the shoulder, which, if it had happened, probably would have done permanent damage to my nervous system. I kept a sharp eye on the house, and in doing so, managed to start plugging up the mower again on a regular basis. A half hour later when I finished, I was drenched in sweat, and it wasn't entirely from the work.

I put the mower away and closed the shed door. Then, feeling that I'd done my duty, I started down the lane toward the road. Halfway there, I turned and studied the house again. Now this would be the kind of scene in a movie where the person would get the idea to go back and check things out and the audience would all be thinking, "No, you idiot! Get out of there while you can!" Only in the movie the audience *knows* there's something strange and deadly going on, and I didn't—not the deadly part anyway. So my curiosity got the better of me (the same as it always does everyone in the movies) and within two minutes I found myself standing at the front door trying to decide whether to go in. Looking down, I noticed the key was already in my hand. Since I hadn't even remembered pulling it out of my pocket, I took this as some kind of a sign. Before I could talk myself out of it, I opened the door.

Daytime or not, I had to admit it felt pretty spooky being in there, and I wished Bo or Jeremy or Pop or somebody had been with me. As I headed slowly toward the staircase, I thought of Clutzy's ghost again—only this time I wasn't laughing.

At first I was kind of tiptoeing up the stairs, and then I decided I might better make a little noise. In case somebody (or some*thing*) *was* there, that'd give him (*it*) a chance to get out of my way. Any way you looked at it, what I was doing didn't make sense. There I was, searching the house to see if I'd find anything, and at the same time making noise so that whatever might be there would hide or sneak out before I found it. Of course, I kept telling myself the place was empty except for me, but the way my heart was racing proved I just wasn't buying it.

I made it to the closed door of Rachel's room without seeing or hearing anything out of the ordinary. I thought about going inside, but decided Andy's room was the one I needed to look at first. Until I'd checked *it* out, I knew, my heart would continue trying to beat its way out through my rib cage.

I moved down the hall slowly, tiptoeing again for some reason even though I'd just decided making noise was safer. The door to Andy's room was closed, which is the way we'd left it. I reached for the knob and turned it in slow motion. Pushing the door open gradually, I scanned the room without stepping into it. Then, by sheer force of will, I leaned in and checked behind the doorway, letting out an audible sigh of relief when I didn't find anything lurking there.

Once in the room I started to feel a little better. Everything looked just the way we'd left it. I went over and looked out the window at the newly mowed lawn. I smiled as I pictured myself down there shaking in my boots, thinking something was watching me from where I now stood. I smiled even more as I thought about the ghost noises Jeremy would have been making if he'd been there with me.

A few minutes later I found myself back at Andy's desk studying his school picture again. This was the third time I'd seen it, and I was really starting to feel as though I knew this kid, and not only just knew him, but kind of liked him too—thinking that if I'd been around when he was growing up we'd probably have been good friends. And even though I'd never even met the guy, I started feeling a little sad—as if I missed him, missed having him around.

I reached again for the picture hanging on the bulletin board above his desk, the one taken out by the old Rexleigh Bridge, and I had the same feeling of sadness all over again, thinking how it would have been nice to have had this pleasant-faced kid for a neighbor, and how he could have shown me about working on cars and like that, and how if he was around now he could have been in our films, and then his life—the way he sounded and looked and reacted to things—would have been somehow preserved. I had a strong feeling he would have fit right in with us and would have gotten a kick out of Rosasharn's antics and Jeremy's sarcasm. I had no reason to believe any of these things except for the few pictures I'd seen and the nice things Pop had said about him, but I believed them nonetheless.

I set the Rexleigh Bridge picture down next to his school picture the way I'd done the day before, and as I compared them one last time a sudden thought hit me like a jolt out of the blue. It dawned on me I'd never put the picture back on the bulletin board the day before. I'd studied it, set it next to the other picture, and then Jeremy'd started talking to me and we'd left. I was *sure* of that. And yet when I showed up today the picture'd been hanging up again. As if someone felt it *belonged* there!

I turned quickly and looked around the room again. Everything still looked the same but . . . I thought for a second. Hadn't Jeremy left that car magazine he'd dug out of the closet on Andy's bed? If he had, it wasn't there now. My eyes went over to the closet, which was open just a crack. That's probably the way it was when I'd walked in, probably the way Jeremy'd left it the day before when he finished scrounging around in there, but I couldn't be sure. All I was sure of was that the snapshot had been moved, and probably the magazine, and that meant I might not be alone. I started to back out of the room, never once taking my eyes off that closet door, ready to take off like a shot if I even *suspected* I saw it move.

Once out in the hallway, I picked up my pace considerably, took the stairs two at a time, hit the door, and was gone.

Seventeen

I was halfway home and still moving at a pretty good clip when Ray McPherson pulled up next to me. "Hey there, Gabey," he said, leaning out his window. "How's she goin'?"

Being called Gabey wasn't high on my list of concerns at the moment. Besides, Ray had called me that my whole life, and it was head and shoulders above Jeremy's "Gabe-boy."

"Not bad," I answered. "How about you?"

"Can't complain," he said, and then followed with, "Don't do no good anyhow. You know what I mean?"

Our conversation continued at about this caliber for a few minutes, and then Ray pulled it around to what he really wanted to talk about. "Tell me something, Gabey. You notice anything squirrelly going on around here lately?"

The question didn't take me totally by surprise, but I still didn't know how to answer it. Ray obviously had in mind Rosasharn's performance on the hood of his car, and as far as I was concerned the further we stayed away from that subject, the better. And as far as opening up to Ray and sharing all the troubling things I'd been noticing lately . . . well, I wasn't up for that either.

"Like what?" I said lamely.

Ray looked up and down the road and off to both sides before saying anything more. "Get in," he said finally. "You heading for home?"

I told him I was and walked around to the passenger side and climbed in. Ray just wasn't the type you said "Thanks, but I'd rather walk" to.

"You hear what happened to me a few weeks ago?" Ray said, kind of making a question out of it and kind of not, as he dropped the shifting lever to "drive" and gave the car some gas.

I nodded, not daring to offer any more than that. For all I knew, he could have already found out that I was one of the ones involved in that whole fiasco and had been cruising my road hoping to catch me alone so he could settle the score.

"Huh?" he said, giving me a poke. At first I thought maybe it was a "You lying to me, boy?" kind of "huh," but then I realized he'd been looking out the window and hadn't seen me nod.

"I heard," I said.

"That sonavabitch was on my car like a cheap suit," he told me. "Ya see the friggin' *dents* it made up there? Check 'em out."

I took that as an order and leaned forward to get a look. You'd have to be more familiar with the various dents scattered around Ray's car than I was to know which were the ones Rosasharn had contributed. Even so, I didn't feel like being implicated in causing *any* of them. After I'd studied the hood for what I thought was the proper amount of time and with the proper look of commiseration, I nodded again.

"Huh?" he said, and gave my arm another poke.

"Yeah," I answered. I sincerely hoped if he was leading up to the notion that those dents would have to be paid for, he was thinking in terms of money, not some kind of physical atonement. I looked over and studied him with quite a bit more interest than I'd studied the hood with. His eyes were still out on surveillance, sweeping across the fields and woods on both sides of us.

"There was two of them sons-o'-bitches," Ray said finally after he'd pulled his passenger wheels onto the lawn in front of my house and for the first time turned his full attention to me. "One of 'em jumped in front of me and then landed on my hood and did that." He jabbed a thumb out toward his hood. "The other one run off into the trees. And with two-to-one odds I figured it was time to barrel-ass outta there, which is exactly what I did, and you'da done the same."

I sat there. As much as I wanted to, it just wasn't the right moment to say "Thanks for the ride" and get out. I looked over and noticed Pop's car wasn't back in the yard yet. No cavalry to the rescue.

"You wanna know what I'm thinking?" Ray said, and looked for all the world as if he were staring right through me.

I nodded—reluctantly.

"I'm thinking them sonavabitchin' things are the same sons-o'-bitches that come charging out of the woods last Saturday at that stupid-assed drug day they was having at that tax drain they call a school."

"Yeah?" I said—not so brilliant, maybe, but then I hadn't had time to plan for this conversation.

Ray wasn't through making connections. "That ain't all," he said. "You know what else I'm thinking?"

I held my breath, waiting for the other shoe to drop.

Ray continued solemnly. "I think John Lindstrom seen 'em too, and that's what give him his stroke. I come prit' near having one myself seeing that numb-nut-looking thing staring down at me . . . nothing between us but a friggin' windshield. I'm telling ya, Gabey, you never seen nothin' like it!" He wore a

vague but undeniable look of pride as he studied me—
the look of a survivor.

"He told Pop he saw his son," I said, hoping to
steer the conversation a little.

"And what's *that* tell you?" Ray said. "You're supposed to be a smart guy. What's that mean in *your*
book?"

I shrugged, not having the slightest idea what he
wanted me to say.

"*College*," he said, kind of disgusted. Not meaning
that I'd gone, but that I was the type who *would* go, and
already I'd lost my common sense. I didn't get all this
out of that one word, but from a whole lifetime of living in Wakefield.

"It *means*," Ray continued in what I took to be his
remedial voice, "that he's crazier than a outhouse rat."
He studied me to see if I was getting his drift. It must
be he didn't think I was because he rolled his eyes and
continued in that same remedial voice. "I've known
John Lindstrom my whole life, and he may have been
missing a few cards, I'll give you that, but you know as
well as I do, most of his friggin' deck was still there.
Until that night." He leaned in toward me. "So you tell
me. What did that sonavabitch see that night that
knocked him over the edge? He *seen* one of them
sorry-assed . . . whatever the hell the friggin' things
are. You can't *tell* me he didn't."

He waited to see if I had any intention of telling
him he didn't.

"And that ain't all," he continued. "There's other
donkey dookie going on around here."

It suddenly came back to me why I'd been
trekking down the road at such a good clip. "Like
what?" I asked, this time genuinely interested.

"Like at that friggin' house you just left," he said.

He definitely had my interest now, and I figured he knew it and was playing it for all the drama he could.

"You see anything in there?" he wanted to know.

I shrugged. "Like what?" I said again, dying to know what he was getting at.

He looked at me and nodded knowingly. "Let's just say that God forsaken dump of a place ain't as empty as it's supposed to be."

I sat up straighter and looked at him. "Yeah?" I said.

"I've seen things," he said importantly. "More than once."

"You've seen things in the house?" My heart started picking up the pace again just from remembering the feeling I'd had when I left there.

He nodded, playing it for all it was worth. "Damn right."

"Pop's been in there," I said, thinking that might be what he saw. "And I've been over a few times with my friends. We cleaned the place one day."

He shook his head. "I ain't talking about your old man, or you and your squirrel-bait friends. Things friggin' happen when you ain't even *close* to that place."

"Yeah?" I said. Guys like Ray always seemed to have a pretty good handle on where everybody is at any given time, which always amazed me since I wasn't even sure where *I* was half the time.

Ray nodded. "At first I thought maybe that pill-faced daughter of his had come back and was staying there. You ever see her? She's scarier than the sonavabitchin' thing that was on my friggin' hood. But I didn't see no car around. And then I find out from Clutzy today that she ain't been here and you couldn't get her here if you wanted to, even though I don't know why anybody'd friggin' want to. So if *she* ain't been here, how do you explain some of the hocus pocus I been seeing? Lights on, then off, shades down, then up, you name it. Then one friggin' afternoon I seen something moving around the living room. And it wasn't you and your brother 'cause you were out in the yard draggin' around that fur ball calf, and your old man was at his office, and young Rosa was cleaning motel rooms and young Wulfson mowing hay and young Michaelson out at the damn country club. So I pull up and look through the friggin' windows, but whatever it was I seen has already made itself good and scarce. I shoulda kicked the sonavabitchin' door down, but at the time I was still thinking it mighta been Rachel and I didn't feel like ending up face-to-face with that. But come to find out it *wasn't* Rachel, and it wasn't Rachel any of them other times either. So I seen you over there again today and I wanted to find out if you knew what in God's green friggin' earth was going on at that place."

I shook my head and probably looked just wide-eyed enough to be believable. "I wish I did."

"I'll tell you something, Gabey—just between you me and the sonavabitchin' man in the moon. I'm about done *wishing* I knew what was goin' on there. Tonight I'm gonna find out for myself."

I looked at him. "Whaddaya gonna do?"

"You ain't gotta worry," he said. "I ain't gonna break into your pal's precious friggin' place. Not unless I have to anyway. But I'll be there watching, you can bet your hindquarters on that, and I'll stay all sonavabitchin' night if I have to."

"And if you see something?"

Ray snorted and reached into his backseat. "Depends. But I might just play me some baseball." He pulled out a beat-up old baseball bat that looked like it might have belonged to Babe Ruth's grandfather and waved it in my face. "This here's Betsy," he told me, "and I wouldn't wanna be some sorry-assed, numb-nutted, green sonavabitch when old Betsy's open for business." He nodded solemnly and looked down at Betsy like a proud father and then back to me. "No sirree, Gabey. I would not."

Eighteen

I hurried in to the phone, hoping I could get hold of everybody before it was too late. We'd planned to meet at the pond to do some more filming that evening, but that no longer seemed like such a bright idea. With Ray and his pal Betsy lurking in the shadows, just itching for action, the last thing we needed was for Rosasharn and Jeremy and Ethan to be running around Mr. Lindstrom's property decked out as creatures from the underworld. Knowing Ray, by evening he'd have downed a few beers, and even if he didn't start clubbing them on sight, we still wouldn't be out of the woods. When it dawned on him that we were responsible for the original attack on his car, it could have a serious impact on his pride, which, in turn, could have a serious impact on *our* well-being—especially mine, since I was the one who'd sat right next to him and listened to him tell the whole cockamamie story without saying a word. And if I didn't call ahead, it'd be just like Rosasharn to put on his stupid costume and go driving down the road right past Ray and then wave to him for good measure. It'd be *Rogue Nun* all over again.

I reached Bo at the pro shop and filled him in. He found a little more humor in the situation than I did but agreed it probably wasn't a good time for the Green family to be out and about. He suggested we still meet at the pond and just make it a night of R & R before our Regents exams. That sounded good to me. Then we'd be close by if Ray did find something, which I half figured he might, based on some of the strange things I'd been seeing around there lately.

Next I called Rosasharn and explained the whole nine yards to him. Then I made him put Sudie on the line so I could fill her in. This was in case Rosasharn saw some comic potential in all this and it clouded his better judgment—assuming Rosasharn had some better judgment to cloud. Sudie said she wouldn't be able to meet us at the pond until later, but she assured me she'd keep Rosasharn's costume under lock and key and that he'd be showing up in civilian clothes—or naked.

I couldn't get hold of Jeremy, but I wasn't too worried about that. Jeremy wasn't the type who'd be likely to be parading around the neighborhood as Green Gal unless Rosasharn orchestrated the whole thing the way he did at the drug day, and since Rosasharn wouldn't have his own costume, that wasn't likely. Or so I figured at the time.

Pop called from the hospital to say that Mr. Lindstrom had taken a turn for the worse and that he and Ethan would stay on for a while to keep track of things and then have dinner in Cambridge. I offered to come over, but Pop said that wouldn't be necessary, that Mr. Lindstrom was resting and it could be days or even weeks before anything happened. The way he said it, I had a pretty good idea what he meant by "anything."

After I hung up the phone, I grabbed my biology book, figuring I'd give studying another try. It didn't work. I kept picturing three things in my mind. The first was Mr. Lindstrom lying there on his hospital bed getting weaker by the minute, knowing—during his conscious moments anyway—that the only family member he had left in the world hated him. Other times I'd see that closet door in Andy Lindstrom's room flying open and some crazy thing I couldn't quite picture charging out at me as I stood there frozen in my tracks. And if those two images weren't enough to distract me on their own, I kept getting this picture of Ray McPherson, bleary-eyed from a couple sixers of beer, reaching for Betsy and heading my way to dish out some justice.

I arrived at Blood Red Pond before everybody else and started reading a book I'd grabbed from my room. It was one of the books I'd read a while back about people dying and coming back to life. I'm not sure why that particular book caught my eye. It may have had something to do with learning that Mr. Lindstrom was going downhill, or it might have been because of Pop mentioning Judgment Day the night I found him listening to the Pogues. Or maybe neither. The fact is I've always been pretty much intrigued by death. Not like Joey Brooner, who when we were in junior high kept a scrapbook with pictures he'd clipped from the papers and *Time* and *Newsweek* of people who'd been gunned down or blown up and things like that. And not like Mrs. Quinby, who thought death was such an unnatural act that if you so much as heard about anybody who'd died, you needed crisis intervention. With me it was more of—I don't know—an amazement, you might call it. The whole idea of dying has to be one of the most amazing and mysterious things in the world, and it's probably one of the reasons I'm so interested in philosophy and religions and all that.

I skimmed through the book till I found the part I was looking for—the moment when the guy supposedly died, struck by a bolt of lightning so intense it actually melted the nails in his shoes. First he felt this excruciating pain, as you might imagine, but then a feeling of peace and tranquility like he'd never felt in his whole life came over him. Somewhere along the line he realized he was above the scene—looking down at his own body—and he watched as his wife desperately tried CPR on him and then as the ambulance guys loaded him onto the stretcher. Somewhere along the line as he was floating up there, it hit him how the body lying on the stretcher below him really had nothing to do with who he actually was—any more than, say, a hotel room he'd stayed in would. And except for feeling sorry for all the turmoil his dying was causing everyone else, he felt totally free and happy.

I was just settling into the part where he was traveling toward what he described as a Being of Light and feeling a thousand times more love and joy than he could ever remember feeling before, when I was pulled back to earth by the sound of what could only be Rosasharn's car heading up the lane toward me. A minute later the car had lugged itself over the crest of the little hill that kept the pond hidden from the road. I shot a casual look its way and actually did one of those double takes, like in the movies. There was Rosasharn behind the wheel wearing a big goofy smile, and on the passenger side, not wearing any kind of smile was Green Gal, sitting there for all the world to see. I couldn't believe it.

I tore over to the car, yanked Jeremy's door open, and snatched his Green Gal headpiece off. Jeremy may have flashed back to the bee attack from earlier in the weekend because he grabbed the headpiece out of my hand and started swatting me with it.

"Get that costume off!" I yelled at him.

He swatted at me a few more times and then tried to get out of the car. I crammed the door closed on him. Assuming Ray *was* out in the woods someplace watching us, the last thing I wanted him to get was a full body view of Green Gal.

"What's your problem, spaz?" Jeremy said, reaching out through the window and taking a swipe at the side of my head.

"Where are your other clothes?" I said. "What'd you do with 'em?" I managed to duck another swipe while still holding the door closed against him.

Jeremy finally quit trying to push his way out of the car and sat there looking out at me as if I'd gone totally bonkers. "In the back, ya spaz case."

I reached in and grabbed his jeans and shirt which were strewn across the backseat. "Put 'em on," I said, shoving them in through his window. "Come on. Hurry up."

I stood in front of the door, hoping to block the view as much as possible until Green Gal became Jeremy again. From behind me I could hear Jeremy grumbling and grunting as he wrestled his way out of the costume in such close quarters. "First the stupid tub tells me to get into the stupid thing and then spaz boy tells me to get out of it. Somebody oughta make up their mind."

A few minutes later Jeremy's door pushed into my butt and he climbed out and glared at me. "Ya happy now, scrub?"

I breathed a little sigh of relief. He wasn't exactly *GQ* material yet, but at least he looked human again.

"Look, Jeremy," I told him, "Rosasharn was supposed to tell you *not* to wear that stupid costume—unless you like the idea of getting hit across the head with a baseball bat." I filled him in with a few more of the details as Rosasharn looked on smiling and nodding happily.

"You *stupid* tub!" Jeremy said with a fair amount of vehemence after I'd presented enough of the facts so looked at Bo. "I'm surprised you don't believe in ghosts."

"I do," Bo told him.

Jeremy studied him for a moment to see if he was putting him on. "So you think there's a ghost in the house?" he demanded.

"Not really," Bo said. "But I'd like to find out."

"You and me both," I said. "Only tonight isn't the best time to do it."

"Do what?"

I almost jumped a foot in the air. The voice came from what should have been the empty spot right next to me. I turned my head and saw Ethan sitting on the other half of my rock. "Jeez, Ethe. I wish you wouldn't sneak up like that."

"I thought you saw me."

"I *wish*. I oughta put a bell on you or something," I said, poking him.

"We oughta put a bell on your stupid ghost," Jeremy said.

"What ghost?" Ethan looked up and studied my face.

I told him what I'd already told the others about my afternoon and the moved picture and all that. "I was almost sure I saw something in that window," I said. "And I *know* I left that picture down on Andy's desk."

Ethan took all this in without saying anything. But I could tell he was really hashing it over in his mind.

"So what do you think?" I still had a hunch Ethan knew more than he was letting on.

He shrugged. It was the same kind of shrug he'd given the day before when I'd asked him what he thought he saw when he kept looking out into the woods.

"Well, we can't do anything about it tonight anyway," I told him. "Not with Ray McPherson over there snooping around with a baseball bat, just waiting for somebody to make a move."

Ethan glanced up at me. He didn't say anything, but his face had kind of a stricken look to it. Sudie must have thought so too.

"Don't worry," she told him. "Ray won't bother us. Not as long as we're dressed like *people* anyway." She elbowed Rosasharn and gave him a dirty look.

Rosasharn went into his Italian weeping routine. "I maka one mistaka," he wailed. "How longa must I pay for thissa one mistaka?" He raised his fists to heaven and did some more wailing.

I looked over to see if this got a smile out of Ethan. It didn't. He was standing up and looking even more serious than usual. "I think I'll go home," he said, and gave my shoulder a little tap.

"You just got here," I said.

He shrugged apologetically. I waited but he didn't offer any explanation. He gave us his little aloha wave and started walking down the lane.

"He's been acting funny all week," I said as soon as he was out of hearing range.

"Maybe he's a ghost," Jeremy said.

"He's probably a little upset about Mr. Lindstrom," Sudie said. "That's gotta be tough on a kid his age."

"It's more than that," I said. "It's like he's up to something.

"*Ethan?*" Sudie said. "He's more responsible than *we* are."

"I'm following him," I announced, deciding all of a sudden. "This whole thing's driving me crazy."

"You want us to go with you?" Bo asked.

I shook my head. "Thanks. But it'll be hard enough to follow him without . . ." I indicated Jeremy, who was pretending he had a phone up to his head.

"Hello, FBI? This is Gabe-boy Riley. I think my brother is a ghost. I have evidence. He just left our campfire here and said he wanted to go home."

"Hey, Jeremy," I interrupted. "Can you order me a pizza on that thing?"

"Shut up," he told me.

I'd never in my life tailed Ethan before, but I knew it wouldn't be easy. For one thing, Ethan generally travels without making a sound, and I generally don't. Also, Ethan has a natural awareness of things going on around him, which meant I had to keep as quiet as I could *and* keep my distance, which in turn meant that by the time I reached the road Ethan was long gone.

I stood still for a few seconds, listening, but of course it didn't do me any good. I half expected Ethan to tap me on the shoulder right while I was standing there looking up and down the road.

My first impulse was to head north toward my house. I was thinking about how Ethan had been sneaking around there the night before and how different things there had turned up missing. But at the last second I decided to go the other way. Ethan had announced he was leaving right after hearing about Ray being over at Mr. Lindstrom's place, so I figured there was probably a connection. And I definitely didn't like the idea of Ethan being around Mr. Lindstrom's house alone—not with Ray lurking around in the bushes and God knows what lurking in the house.

Halfway to Mr. Lindstrom's house I stopped in my tracks and listened. Since I was on a paved road, I was making pretty good time and didn't want to overtake Ethan by accident if that was the direction he'd gone in.

I didn't hear anything and I couldn't make out any movement in the road ahead of me, so I continued on. A few minutes later I was approaching the place. The first time I looked out across the field toward the house I didn't see anything, and I felt a small sense of relief. That didn't last long. After taking a few more steps, I could see a crack of light coming from an upstairs window; it had been blocked by the old box elder at first. I crouched down and tried to decide what to do. Remembering how I'd run out of there that afternoon in broad daylight, I wasn't eager to go sneaking down the driveway at night, especially since I didn't know for sure if Ethan had even come this way. Then there was the Ray problem. I hadn't seen his car yet, but that didn't mean anything; there were any number of places where he could have pulled off into fields, and it was dark enough so I could have walked right by his car without seeing it. For all I knew he was crouched behind me in the ditch, watching me and telling Betsy to get ready for some action.

By now every part of me wanted to leave, but I couldn't do it—not till I made sure Ethan wasn't right in the middle of whatever it was that was going on there. Straining as hard as I could to hear anything unusual, I started easing my way down the driveway, keeping my eye mostly on that sliver of light, which I was now pretty sure was coming from Andy's room, but also stopping and scanning the darkness around me from time to time. The whole situation gave me the creeps, and I was wishing I'd at least let Bo come with me.

Halfway down the lane I cut left into the hayfield. It was quieter (but wetter) going through the hay, and it gave me a more dead-on look at the front of the house. The sliver of light was still there, and I could see now that it was definitely coming from Andy's room. I crouched in the tall grass for a few minutes and watched to see if I could make out any kind of movement up there. I couldn't. Then I scanned the yard and didn't see any movement there either, so I started edging forward again, a little slower and more cautiously as I got closer.

A minute later I learned firsthand the meaning of the phrase "all hell broke loose." It started with a loud crack which I didn't realize was a gunshot until a little later. Next I heard a voice shout "Son of a *bitch!*" and some crashing sounds from inside the house. I hadn't even realized the front door had been open until a figure came charging out of it. He was carrying a flashlight and, from the movement of the beam, I'd guess he did a complete forward roll before coming to his feet and heading lickety-split down the driveway. It was only then that I realized the voice I'd heard was Ray's, which probably meant he was the person retreating too. My head was peeking out over the top of the tall grass taking in the whole scene when another crack rang out through the night, this time followed by a Fourth-of-July-firecracker whistling noise which was coming my way. I'd never been on the receiving end of a gun before, but I instinctively recognized the sound of a bullet whizzing past and hit the dirt with my hands covering my head, as if that would have done any good. Next I heard Ray's voice again, farther down the driveway now and more frantic than ever.

"Start the friggin' car, Clutz, ya dumb son of a bitch!"

From the pace of the footsteps it was easy to tell that these words were delivered at a full gallop. The car roared to life and, judging by the sound, it couldn't have been hidden far from where I'd turned off the driveway into the hayfield. A door slammed shut, then the car bucked and stalled once, started again, and tore off for the road. It made a decent screech as it hit the pavement and gunned its way north.

With the car gone everything seemed deadly silent. I slowly rose to my knees and peeked out, careful not to raise my head much above the tall grass. One thing I knew—I never wanted to hear the sound of a bullet sizzling that close to me again. As I watched, the shade in Andy's room pulled back slightly and a figure peered out the window. As a reflex I scrunched tighter into the hay, although there was no way anybody could have seen me in the dark from that far away. A few seconds later the shade drooped down again, leaving nothing but the sliver of light. My head floated back up out of the hay.

What happened next scared me more than hearing the bullet or seeing the guy in the window. A figure came out from behind the old box elder and glided silently toward the house. It paused for a second at the top of the stoop and then disappeared through the doorway.

There was no doubt about who it was. I only knew one person who moved that way, and he was just the right size too.

Ethan was in that house now.

Nineteen

I came skulking out of my hideaway and headed toward the front door. When I reached the freshly mowed lawn, I crouched for a few seconds and studied the house—first the upstairs room with the light on and next the open doorway downstairs. Nothing had changed. I did a little quick and silent sprint until I was on the front stoop, then stood there trying to quiet my breathing. The last thing I wanted to do was go inside, but I had no choice. My mind was cranking out one message to the rhythm of my pounding heart. *Ethan is in there. Ethan is in there.*

I stepped inside and listened. Nothing. I didn't expect to hear Ethan but had hoped I'd hear *something*. When you're in this kind of situation and you know you're not alone, it's better to hear things than not to hear them. Trust me on this one.

I started creeping toward the staircase, easing into each step, trying almost to *think* myself across the old floor without having it creak. Surprisingly, I made it without a sound. I tried the same thing as I climbed onto the first stair and made that without a sound too.

I couldn't be sure Ethan had even gone upstairs, but if he hadn't, at least I'd be putting myself between him and whatever the trouble was up there, and if he had . . . well, I'd want to be there too.

I was halfway up the stairs when I heard the voice. It was coming from above me and it wasn't Ethan's—or anybody else's I recognized.

"Get out!" The voice was shaking with intensity. "Go away. I don't want you here!"

For a second I thought it was talking to me, and I froze in my tracks. Then I realized it was talking to somebody else—somebody I couldn't hear.

"I don't care!" the voice said. "It's too late. Don't you get it? It's *too late!*"

I don't remember starting to move again, but I found myself almost to the top of the staircase. I had a pretty good idea who the person I couldn't hear was.

"NO, NO, NO!" The voice was really shouting now. "I told you it's too *late.* It's over!" Then, "Don't come any closer! I'm warning you!"

"No! *Don't!*"

There was no mistaking *that* voice, and I was already tearing down the hall.

"No!" Ethan shouted again. "Don't do it!"

I made the last few steps almost without touching the floor, it seemed, and charged through the open door.

And froze dead in my tracks.

I *saw* it, but I couldn't believe it. Right in front of me, as big as life, was *Andy Lindstrom!* And if that weren't shock enough to kill me on the spot, he had the shotgun Jeremy had found in the closet and it was aimed right into his own mouth.

The guy—Andy—looked as shocked to see me as I was to see him, if that's possible, and he pulled the gun out and leveled it at me. I wasn't even aware of Ethan until he stepped out in front of me—between me and the gun—and stood there holding his arm out at Andy.

"*No,*" he said. "Put it down."

It took me a few seconds to come to my senses enough to remember why I'd come into the house in the first place. When I did, I grabbed Ethan by the shoulders and tried to pull him behind me. He reached back and snagged on to my shirt. Then he locked his arms and wouldn't budge. I didn't think the two of us getting into a wrestling match would help the situation any, so I let up. Ethan still had two tight fistfuls of my shirt.

For a minute, I stood there looking over Ethan's head at the guy—at Andy—still not sure which shocked me more: the sight of *him* or the sight of the gun. The thing was, he was actually *younger* than he was when he supposedly died. The kid standing in front of me couldn't have been any older than I was, if that. And yet I'd looked at that picture of Andy enough to recognize the face, even though the face staring me down now wasn't wearing any shy grin.

"What are you doing here?" I said, when I was finally able to talk.

"What am *I* doing here?" he said as if he couldn't believe his ears. "What about *you?*" He waved the gun our way.

It didn't do my heart any good to see him using his gun to point, especially since we were the ones he was pointing at. It was probably a slug from that thing that had whistled over my head earlier. "I'm a friend of your father's," I stammered out, still too much in shock to fully grasp that I was probably explaining myself to a ghost.

"You're *lying,*" he said, taking a few steps toward me. "You don't even know my father."

I wasn't about to start an argument with anybody—even a ghost—who had a gun pointed at me, so I just stood there.

"*Andy,*" Ethan said, "it's my brother. He won't hurt you." It seemed funny that he was telling a guy with a gun—let alone a guy who was supposed to be dead already—that I wouldn't hurt *him.*

"You *know* this guy?" I said, kind of turning Ethan around so I could see his face.

He loosened his grip on my shirt and nodded. "It's Andy Foster. I met him a few days ago."

"Andy *Foster?*" As if I wasn't confused enough to begin with.

Ethan nodded again. "He's Mr. Lindstrom's grandson."

If it's possible to feel like a total fool at the same time as you're more scared than you've ever been in your life, I did. I should have guessed it was something like that. I knew firsthand how traits could stick with a family, even a few generations down the line. The first time I ever saw a picture of Pop's uncle Seamus as a kid, I almost fell over. He could have been my twin brother. It was the same thing with Ethan and my mother's father. So that explained why I thought the kid was Andy Lindstrom. But that was *all* it explained.

I looked at Andy again—this new, though not necessarily improved, Andy. "So what's the deal here?" The words sounded a lot more rational and self-assured than I felt.

"The deal is, you're leaving," he said.

"Fine by me." I was already starting to back up when I felt Ethan's grip tighten on my shirt again.

"*No,*" he said with as much urgency as I'd ever heard from him. "We can't. He's gonna *shoot* himself!" He looked up at me. He was almost crying, but his face was so trusting—as if he really believed I could do something about the situation. "You gotta talk to him," he said.

My eyes flicked back across the room to where

Andy was waiting, almost patiently, you might say, for whatever I might have up my sleeve. But try as I might, the only thing I could come up with to say was, "Would you mind pointing the gun somewhere else?"

He studied me as if trying to decide what I was capable of, which obviously turned out to be not much. After a few seconds he lowered the gun. "Try something and you *will* regret it," he said in a low voice. "I don't have anything to lose."

Seeing the gun pointing at the floor was at least the beginning of a big load off my mind. "All right," I said. "All right. That's good." I had my hands up over Ethan's shoulders and I was doing some kind of an everybody-just-stay-calm thing with them. Andy got calm enough to roll his eyes. Ethan waited patiently for me to say something intelligent.

"Okay . . . ," I continued. "So . . . I'm Gabe Riley. You already know Ethan, I guess. We're friends of your . . . your grandfather."

The kid watched me babble on. I was almost hoping he'd tell me to shut up. He didn't.

"Sooo . . . ," I continued. "What's the . . . uh . . ." I realized I'd already tried that one, so I switched to "When did you get here?" Even in the middle of all the confusion, it was beginning to dawn on me that his presence went a long way toward explaining what had been going on lately. It probably helped that he was wearing my rugby shirt, and his jeans looked pretty familiar too. Something else dawned on me: Mr. Lindstrom *hadn't* lost his mind. He'd seen this Andy too, and I wouldn't be surprised if that's what gave him his stroke. As far I knew, he didn't even know he *had* a grandson.

Andy looked me over a little more before deciding

whether or not to bother answering my question. "I got here a couple of weeks ago," he said finally. "The night that goofy kid jumped on the guy's car."

"And . . . ?" My calm-down hands were already getting a little impatient, and they were motioning for him to pick up the pace. I pulled them down to my sides before they got us into trouble.

Andy looked down at the floor, and at first I thought he'd said all he was going to say. Then he took a deep breath. "I didn't know what to do at first, so I hid in the woods until I could decide. I saw you guys camped by the pond and started watching you, and then I followed you when you went out to the road."

That probably explained what Ray saw right before Rosasharn landed on his hood. But there was still a lot it didn't explain. "If you came here to see your grandfather, why were you . . . I don't know . . . sneaking around like that?"

He shrugged. "I wanted to watch him for a while. I wanted to see what he was like."

"Didn't it ever occur to you to just knock on his door and introduce yourself?"

"*Listen* to him, Gabe," Ethan said. "He's had a hard time." He was still standing in front of me, but he'd dropped the death grip on my shirt.

I looked at him in surprise. Not because he was sticking up for a guy who was holding us both at bay with a shotgun, but because this was the closest Ethan had ever come to giving me any kind of lip. He came around beside me and patted my arm.

"Go ahead," he said to Andy.

"That guy . . . my grandfather . . . He was my last hope." Andy's voice broke on the word "hope" and his face, which been hard and angry, started to break a little too. He slumped down on the floor by the window. He tried his best not to, but he was starting to cry. He leaned back into the wall with the gun across his lap.

I felt sorry for him, but I was still pretty much occupied being worried about Ethan and me. All while I waited for Andy to continue I was staring at the gun in his lap.

He took a couple of big snuffs and then went on. "I had to go someplace. I couldn't stay home anymore, and this was the only place I could think of." He ran his hand through his hair and shook his head slowly. "My mother . . . she's lost it. All she talks about these days is *him*—about how everything that goes wrong is *his* fault."

My mind was working overtime trying to connect the dots. "Him" had to be her father, Mr. Lindstrom.

"Not that *that's* anything new," he continued. "A couple of years ago, we moved from Maryland back to Saratoga, and I swear she did it just to be near him. So she could bother him. She used to get her loser boyfriend—the loser boyfriend she had at the time—to call his house. As soon as the old guy picked up the phone, the loser would say things like, 'We're watching you' and 'You can run but you can't hide,' that kind of crap. Just to do a number on his head. One time she even made a tape of her loser boyfriend's voice saying that stuff so that she could call him and play it, and meanwhile the loser's over in his yard shooting little pebbles at his windows. When the old guy came charging out, there was a note taped to his porch that said WE *TOLD* YOU WE WERE WATCHING. They pulled that one twice before that loser took off on her. Then we moved to Syracuse with her new loser, and she had him make a few calls from there."

I thought about Mr. Lindstrom sitting alone in that big old house, getting those calls and figuring every time that there was somebody outside spying on him. No wonder he took to ranting and raving around his yard.

"Her latest boyfriend was the worst of the bunch—one of those wheeler-dealer types who's always got something going only he always screws it up. He said he was gonna start some kind of business—cleaning pools or something like that—and he just needed some money to get it off the ground. So my mother gave him all the money we had—about seven hundred dollars. That same night he got busted for cocaine possession—seven hundred dollars' worth. The first guy he tried to sell to turned out to be an undercover cop. So much for his *pool-cleaning* business. The loser." He shook his head some more. "That was the last straw for my mother. No money. No boyfriend. A job she hated. She cried all that night and kept asking over and over what we were gonna do. I tried to talk to her but it was as if she didn't even know I was there."

He paused and almost seemed to drift off for a while. An uncomfortable silence filled the room, but for the life of me I couldn't think of a thing to say.

"When I was little," Andy continued in a voice that sounded weaker and more distant, "I always liked stories about kids living on farms. I always kind of envied those kids. It seemed like such a good life—staying in one place and having animals and lots of land and all that. That night, while my mother was crying nonstop in the next room, I kept thinking about being on a farm. Finally I made up my mind, and I went and told her that we should come here—that however bad she thought her father was, he couldn't be any worse than most of the loser boyfriends we'd lived with."

"What'd she say?" I finally asked after he'd sat slumped there a while without saying anything.

His head came up slowly. He was all-out crying now and didn't even try to hold it back. "She went *crazy*—screaming and throwing stuff and hitting me. . . . She said she'd done the best she could and if that's the way I felt to get the hell out. I guess that night was the last straw for me too because that's just what I did. I didn't even pack anything. I just walked out the door." He took a deep breath. "I slept in a park that night and then started for here. It took me almost the whole next day to hitchhike this far, and then a few more hours to find the place."

"I still don't get why didn't you knock on the door and introduce yourself," I said, but a little nicer than I'd said it before.

Andy shrugged. "All my life I'd heard nothing but bad things about that guy. One other time, when I was little, I'd asked my mother about him, and she slapped me across the face for even mentioning him." He shook his head. "That's a laugh. She's spent her whole *life* talking about him, and I get slapped for just bringing him *up*. Anyway, I couldn't even imagine what he must be like. So when I finally got here, I wasn't all that eager to go running up to the house. I walked around in the woods, thinking about what to do, and that's when I heard you guys. And after the goofy kid jumped on that car, I doubled back around and found stuff to eat at your campsite. The next day, I started getting things I needed from your house."

"So you just walked in and helped yourself?" I was surprised how much that bothered me. My whole life our house had been the kind of place people could feel free to drop in to, and lots of times we'd get home and find Rosasharn or Jeremy or somebody in the living room watching TV. But that was different from having a stranger sneaking in and scrounging around for whatever he felt like helping himself to.

"What'd you *want* me to do? If you don't like it, why don't you try locking your doors once in a while? What are you worried about anyway? It's not like you can't afford to lose a little stuff."

"I don't think that's the point," I said.

"You try being someplace with no money and no place to stay sometime and then come and tell me about the *point*." He let that sink in before continuing. "I moved into here after the old guy got sent to the hospital. Your brother heard me in your kitchen a few nights ago picking up some things. The last few days he's been getting me what I needed."

I realized that he'd probably been in our house practically every day up until when Ethan found him. He'd even been picking up fresh clothes and leaving the dirty clothes in the laundry pile, for crying out loud.

"He saw you, didn't he?" I said. "Your grandfather. He saw you the night he had the stroke."

Andy nodded. "That night . . . I'd finally decided to speak to him. . . . After he'd backed the tractor into that old barn, I walked up to the door . . ." He was back to crying again, almost as hard as before. "He saw me in the doorway. . . . At first he just stared at me, and then he started coming at me. I've never seen that kind of look on anybody's face. . . . I knew then my mother was right about him. The next thing I know he's chasing me. The crazy old man is chasing me, waving his arms and yelling for me to come back. I ran all the way to the pond and hid out. There was no way I was gonna let that head case get his hands on me. Then the next morning the ambulance was there. I didn't know something had happened to him, but it didn't matter. He was crazy anyway." He pulled my rugby shirt up to wipe his eyes.

"He wasn't crazy," I said. "He thought you were the *other* Andy. His son." I pointed to the picture on the desk.

He gave a sneering laugh. "And that's not crazy? He thought I was some kind of a zombie? Yeah, he sounds like he's all there." He wiped his eyes on my shirt again and looked over at me looking at him. "What? You want your precious shirt back? You can have it."

He reached down and grabbed the bottom of the shirt. For a second I thought he was going to pull the shirt up over his head and throw it at me, and when he did I was going to charge him—hit him in the midsection and tackle him when his head was covered and his arms were tangled in the sleeves. Ethan might not like it, I knew, but once I had the gun I'd feel better about things. He didn't do it though. He wiped his eyes again and let the bottom of the shirt fall back down. "You can get it tomorrow," he said bitterly. "I won't be needing it."

That seemed to remind him of what he intended to do. He took the gun off his lap and kind of waved it our way. "Look, I don't want to hurt you, but you gotta get going. That jerk with the bat is probably crying to the police right now about me shooting at him, and I'm not waiting around for them to come and get me." There was a hitch in his voice as he said this, then his eyes went down to the gun. A tear ran down his cheek, and he wiped it away angrily. "Just go, will ya?"

"Why don't you come with us?" I said, kind of surprised to hear myself saying it. "You don't have any-place to go, and—"

"That's right!" he said angrily. "I don't have any-place to go! This was the last chance I had. I don't even care anymore. I'm not going back home, and *he's* his-tory. Even if he wasn't crazy, which he *is*, he's not get-ting out of that hospital. I've heard you talking about him. He's gonna die."

I shrugged. "Maybe. But he's not crazy. It was just the shock of seeing you. That and . . . Did you know your mother was suing him?"

He nodded. "Something she picked up from one of her afternoon talk shows. Watching those is another of her specialties—in addition to hooking up with worthless guys." He wasn't crying now. He just looked tired. "I'm so sick of it," he said. "I'm sick of everything. It doesn't even matter anymore. That old guy—he's a goner. And my mother might as well be, with the way she lives." He was quiet for a few seconds, and then he started crying again. "Coming here was my last hope. And look how it turned out." He slammed his free hand into the wall angrily. "So get out of here!" he yelled with a sudden violent intensi-ty. "Get out! Do you want to see this? Do you want your little brother to see this? Go on! Get!"

The gun barrel was up to his mouth again. His fin-ger was on the trigger, and his hand was shaking like mad. He'd gone hysterical.

"Don't!" I yelled, and Ethan did too. It all of a sud-den dawned on me that that's what Ethan had been yelling at him when I arrived, and that my arrival had just delayed things a few minutes. "Your grandfather . . . ," I stammered. "We don't know for sure he won't pull through. You can at least wait and see."

He pulled the gun back a few inches. "Last

chance," he said in a deadly quiet voice. "You'd better leave." The gun went back to his mouth.

I'd like to think I would have kept talking—that I would have said all the right things and saved the day. But I'm not sure I could have said anything more. I'll never know. Because just then we heard Pop's voice calling us from downstairs. Andy lowered the gun and leaned his head back against the wall and just stayed like that for the longest time with his eyes closed. I think I felt sorrier for him at that moment than at any other. I knew he had to be thinking that even his suicide wasn't coming out right. It would have been the perfect time to rush him, but I just stood there with Ethan, feeling terrible, but relieved too that Pop was here to take control of things. I could hear Pop making his way up the stairs, asking if we were cleaning the upstairs now or what. I finally managed to yell, "In here, Pop," although he would have found us anyway since Andy's room was the only one with a light on.

Ethan and I stayed where we were as Pop headed down the upstairs hallway toward us. "Sudie and the boys said I might find you here," he was saying. "I got a call from the hospital and I'm afraid things aren't looking so good with John."

I looked at Andy. He was still leaning against the wall, the gun back in his lap, as he waited, resigned to the whole thing, for Pop to enter the room.

"We'd better step lively—" Pop stopped in midstep and midsentence when he saw Andy on the other side of the room. He seemed to study him for a few seconds, his jaw hanging down. "Well, I'll be dipped and fried," he finally said. He took a few steps closer and studied Andy some more. "For a second I could have sworn I was seeing a ghost, but that's not the case, now is it?"

"Don't bother coming any closer," Andy said wearily. "God, you people might as well move into this house."

Pop looked from Andy to us and then back to Andy. "The resemblance is simply *remarkable*," Pop said. "Simply remarkable."

Andy didn't say anything more, so I started filling Pop in on some of the details, tentatively at first and then picking up some steam when Andy didn't try to stop me. Ethan looked up at me a few times and nodded, in silent appreciation, I think, of the way I was summing things up.

Pop listened to the whole spiel, making the usual Pop sounds and facial expressions, studying Andy and shaking his head in wonder. "Well, I'll be dipped and fried," he said again when I'd pretty much wrapped up the story.

"So *now* you'll get out?" Andy said, waving the gun feebly toward the door.

"Yes," Pop told him. "And you will too. You're coming to the hospital with us."

As soon as he took a step in Andy's direction, the gun went back up to Andy's head. "I'll do it right in front of you," he said. "Right in front of all of you, so don't fool with me. Just get going!" His finger was shaking on the trigger.

"You'll do no such thing," Pop said. "Look, son, if you're determined to kill yourself, there's nobody can stop you. There'll be plenty of time for that later—there's always later for that sorry kind of business. But right now there's a man in the hospital, somebody who means a lot to us and I think would mean a lot to you if you knew him. He lost his son to an accident, and his daughter to"—he waved his hand—"to God knows what, and if I can show him his grandson before he leaves this earth, then dammit, I'm gonna do it. Now, for the love of Peter, do the decent thing and put that gun down and come with us."

"I don't owe *him* anything," Andy said. "What's he ever done for me?"

"He's your *grandfather!*" Pop said as if that explained it all, and maybe it did. "So you'll have to put your personal plans on hold for a few hours. After he's gone, I'll bring you back here and if you still have it in your head that you want to do away with yourself, I won't stop you. You have my word."

Andy thought about that. "How do I know you're telling the truth?"

Pop took a couple of steps closer. "Now, son, I've done a lot of things in my life, and many of them not so good. But one thing I've *never* been guilty of is looking someone straight in the eye and telling a lie." He waved his hand and seemed to think for a few seconds. "I will, however, admit to trotting out a few *spectacular* ones with averted eyes."

It was that little follow-up that did it, I think—the kind Pop was so good at and I'd seen him use so many times in court to bring a smile not only to the jury and the gallery, but to the judge as well. Andy lowered the gun, and before it even reached his lap, Pop had it in one hand and had his other hand on Andy's shoulder.

Andy stood up and Ethan and I followed the two of them out the door.

Twenty

Our ride to the hospital was an experience in itself. Pop was doing a superb juggling act, sending a steady stream of conversation Andy's way to get him settled down while at the same time making better time on the road than I ever hope to make again.

He started in on Andy before we'd even made it to the end of Mr. Lindstrom's driveway. "I don't know how much you know about your grandfather, but before you see him I think there's a few things, at least, you ought to know."

Andy sneered. "Now you're gonna tell me how great he is—or *was*. Save your breath. I know as much about him as I wanna know."

Pop whipped the car onto the road and after straightening it out looked at him. "I was planning nothing of the sort. Whenever anybody describes someone as being *great*, you can bet there's a fair amount of fiction mixed in with the facts. The same is true on the other side, I expect. I'll start with something you probably already know. Your grandfather could be a *son* of a gun, and, God willing, he still is. And *pigheaded?* In that category he simply has no equal, as I'm sure a few of the nurses at the hospital would be more than willing to testify. He could be, without a doubt, the most ornery, crotchety person you'd ever want to—"

"I get the idea," Andy said, cutting him off. "God, you go on about things."

"Yes . . . ," Pop said thoughtfully as we screeched onto the main road. "Someone once told me that, I think . . . can't remember who right now." He paused a few seconds as if he were trying to come up with a name, which was pure theatrics because he knew perfectly well it could have been any judge who'd ever heard one of his cases and half of all the people he'd ever talked to. "Anyway," he said, seeming to snap out of it, "your grandfather, *great?* I don't know about that. But he was a good man. *Yes,* he was," he said, as if expecting an argument. "For whatever flaws he had, he was a decent man and one who loved—loves—his kids. For crying out loud, he even loves *my* kids."

"Yeah, right. And that's why my mother's suing his ass."

Pop nodded. "Suing his ass because he paddled hers, as I understand it. Would that be a fair summation?"

"She told me he never had a kind word for her in her whole life."

"A kind word, did you say? Is *that* what she wanted? Well, yes, she was barking up the wrong tree if she expected that. Kind words aren't John Lindstrom's stock-in-trade. No, sir. But after she left, I saw him poring over catalogs, driving to Albany, Saratoga, Glens Falls . . . searching for that perfect Christmas gift, birthday gift, whatever—the thing he hoped might make her happy—and then he'd wrap it with those big clumsy hands of his and send it on to her. This is when he still knew where she was. And he never did find out about you. To this day he doesn't know you exist."

"I tried to say something to him," Andy said. "He saw me and started going crazy."

"He thought it was his *son,*" I said from the back

in case Pop hadn't put that together yet.

Pop nodded and looked at Andy. "I thought as much. You're the spittin' image of your uncle Andy; you may already know that. When your grandfather spotted you, he must have thought for sure he was seeing things."

The amazing thing was, while Pop was carrying on this whole conversation, he was doing some truly spectacular driving. In fact, in the end I was never sure if it was Pop's gift for gab that began to turn Andy around or if it was his driving, which could have functioned as a kind of shock therapy. I couldn't believe it myself. Pop's always been superb at driving home a point, but I'd never known he had any special talents behind the wheel. I'd heard a few stories over the years from people who knew Pop way back when about what a live wire he'd been, but that was a Pop from the past and not one I ever expected to come face-to-face with. Ethan and I sat in the backseat with our jaws hanging down, and if we hadn't been strapped in, we'd've slid from one side of the car to the other three or four different times.

"Hold on to your hats for this one, boys," Pop instructed before going into one hard corner. "We're flying on a wing and a prayer."

Ethan was the only one wearing a hat, but he didn't take Pop's advice literally any more than I did. We both grabbed the back of the front seats. Andy grabbed his armrest and the console. We didn't need to worry. Pop sailed through the corner as if he'd spent his whole life on the NASCAR circuit.

Halfway to Cambridge, we noticed flashing lights coming up in back of us, and Pop reluctantly pulled off to the side. The flashing lights whipped in behind us.

"It's a state boy, Pop," I said after making out the blue-and-gold Chevy in our taillights. The trooper climbed out slowly and approached our car cautiously, his hand feeling for his gun, expecting, probably, to find a bunch of kids joyriding in a stolen Mercedes. I'm sure his eyes must have gone wide when Pop's gray-haired head poked out from the driver's-side window.

"Stevie," Pop rasped out, "I'm glad it's you. We have to get this boy to the hospital right away!" Luckily Pop knew most of these guys from the courthouse.

"My God," the trooper said. "I *thought* it looked like your car, Mr. Riley, but . . ." Then he snapped out of his daze. He probably figured if Pop was driving like *that,* somebody in the car must be dying. "Follow me," he said, tightening his hat on his head and trotting back to his car.

Following the trooper, even with his flashing lights, actually had the effect of slowing us down. "Don't be timid, Stevie," Pop instructed through the windshield as he bore down on the troop car's bumper. "I'm with you." We kept up with this reverse chase scene all the way to the hospital, the trooper electing to pick up speed rather than risk getting nudged by Pop's bumper. After we'd climbed the winding hill up to the hospital, we split off from him as he raced for the emergency room and we raced for the main entrance. I turned and saw his brake lights and then his backup lights as he realized he'd lost us. I can only guess what his reaction was when he saw all four of us get out of the car and tear into the hospital under our own steam.

After the elevator door closed behind us, I told Pop how impressed I was with his driving.

"Aaaah," he said, waving off the compliment.

Then as an afterthought, "Those Germans can still build a car, now can't they?" He roared out his trademark laugh and threw his arm over my shoulders.

Mr. Lindstrom was a couple of shades paler than the last time I'd seen him and, as far as I could tell at first, not even conscious. But when Pop took a seat next to his bed and picked up his hand, asking if he could hear him, I saw Mr. Lindstrom's hand give Pop's a feeble squeeze.

"I've brought you something, John," Pop said, patting his hand gently, "and you'd better brace yourself for this one." He got up and led Andy over to the bed. "John, meet your grandson, Andy."

I don't know if Mr. Lindstrom caught the "grandson" part or not. But I do know that when he opened his eyes and saw Andy looking down at him, a definite change came over him. It must have been all in his eyes because the rest of his face, his whole face now and not just one side, was as unchanging as a mask. "Eeen," was all he could say, but I knew what it meant. His eyes watered a little as Pop guided Andy into the chair by the bed.

"Andy, this is your grandpa," Pop told him.

Andy didn't say a word. He just sat there and stared down at his grandfather.

It was three hours later before anything happened. Earlier, after Pop had explained to Trooper Stevie what the deal was and Stevie had gone back to his appointed rounds, I'd gone out and moved the car from the main entrance to the parking lot. A couple of times Ethan and I had gone out for hot chocolate and to get coffee for Pop and a soda for Andy. Andy hadn't budged from the bedside. Pop hadn't either, except for stepping out to have that short meeting with the trooper. He'd pulled up a chair next to Andy's and there they sat, hour after hour. Mr. Lindstrom had drifted off to sleep after the first hour as near as I could tell, and most of the time the only sound in the room was his deep, labored breathing. About an hour after midnight, we noticed a change. Each breath now seemed like a struggle, and for a while I thought each one might be his last. This went on for what seemed like forever but was probably only about forty-five minutes. Then all of a sudden I sat up, aware of a strange silence in the room. I was pretty sure what that meant.

Mr. Lindstrom lay there completely still on the bed. Except for the silence and stillness of his chest, he looked the same as he'd looked all along. His face was still a mask. His eyes were closed.

I looked over at Ethan, who was sitting at the foot of the bed, and wondered how he was taking all of this. His eyes were fixed on the ceiling right above Mr. Lindstrom. At first I thought he was deliberately looking away, and I couldn't blame him. This was the first time either of us had ever been around anybody who was dying and it was a little eerie, especially, I figured, for a kid his age. But he didn't appear scared, or even as if he were about to cry, so I thought maybe he'd managed to drift off into his own little world of Superman and magical powers and people who could fly. My eyes went over to Pop, who had reached out and was now holding Mr. Lindstrom's hand. Andy had his arms folded across his chest and was leaning over the bed, almost doubled over as if he had a wicked stomachache. You could tell he was about to cry and didn't want to. I looked back at Ethan again. His eyes were still on the ceiling, but different from before. This time he was more alert, and his eyes were wide and focused. I looked where he was looking but couldn't see anything, which was par for the course. My eyes had just gone back to Ethan when I saw something that sent a tingle up my spine. With his gaze still fixed up there, his face gradually broke into a shy smile. Then he gave his little wave—his aloha wave.

Suddenly it hit me. I looked up again and tried my best to see what Ethan saw. I couldn't, but it didn't matter. I knew what he'd seen. I'd believed it when I read about it, but not the way I believed it at that moment. I felt a kind of exhilaration sweep over me as I thought about Mr. Lindstrom up there, feeling lighter and freer and happier than he'd ever felt in his whole life.

The other part is harder to describe, and I can't swear it wasn't caused by my own thoughts at the time or maybe because I was so tired. All I know is that the experience was real. The tingle I'd felt travel up my spine continued to grow. It spread out across my head until my whole scalp was tingling, and then spread through my face and neck and into my chest. At that moment I felt an almost indescribable peace coming over me. It seemed to be pouring *into* my heart and spreading *out* from my heart at the same time. I touched my arm and felt a delicious tickling sensation, as if my skin was experiencing a joy of its own and sending the good word out to the rest of me. I never knew I could feel so good, let alone at the deathbed of someone who'd been nothing but kind to me my entire life, not to mention this being right on the heels of one of the scariest experiences of my entire life. The whole thing was surreal.

I looked down at Mr. Lindstrom lying on the bed.

Somewhere along the line a nurse had entered the room and was using a stethoscope to check for a heartbeat. "I think it's over," she said softly to Pop.

Pop, still holding Mr. Lindstrom's hand and suddenly looking extremely tired, nodded. Then he folded Mr. Lindstrom's hand gently over the one resting on his chest and gave both hands a final squeeze. "God be with you, John," he said. He reached over and set his hand on Andy's knee. "Would you like a few moments alone, son?"

Andy nodded slowly, and as he did a single tear rolled down his cheek. Pop stood and, wrapping his hand around Andy's neck, pulled Andy's head into him and ruffled his hair. Then gathering Ethan under one arm and me under the other, he led us out of the room.

Twenty-one

Katie and her friend Heather were hanging around the hallway outside the auditorium when I left school Monday afternoon. I think they'd been there for a while because it had been close to a half hour since they'd left the gymnasium, which is where most of our final exams were given. Luckily I hadn't known that Katie was in the gymnasium taking her own test, a few rows over and about ten rows back, until she was handing in her paper, or it would have been a real distraction for me. I had my hands full with the biology Regents as it was.

I didn't see them standing there until I was almost alongside them, which was just as well, because if I'd seen them sooner, I would have been a lot more self-conscious as I approached and might have ended up doing something graceful like tripping over my own feet. I might not have noticed them at all except that my ears happened to pick up a whispered snippit of conversation.

"*Say* something to him."

That's when I glanced over, and that's when it hit me. The thing was, the voice I'd heard was *Heather's*. Was it possible that I'd been mistaken all along and *Katie* was the one who liked me? Those times I'd seen Heather giving me the once-over, had she been doing it on Katie's behalf?

As I rounded the corner and hit the steps toward the side door, my eyes flicked back to where they were standing and I knew it was true. Katie looked stricken and her face silently pleaded with Heather not to blurt out anything else. My heart did a flip and my feet felt light as I glided out the door.

I thought about it a lot, but I didn't actually call her till a few days ago. At first I'd been busy helping Pop with Mr. Lindstrom's wake and funeral, not to mention doing battle with the rest of my exams. Then Katie's family went away on vacation, and then I went to Maine with the Michaelsons, and then—well, I finally made the call. We're planning to go to a movie on Friday and, as near as I can tell, I'm still in love. This may turn out to be a record for me.

Pop managed somehow to smooth things over with Ray, who'd threatened both legal and Betsy action against Andy for the hail of bullets he claimed almost took him out that night. Of course, I happen to know for a fact there were only two bullets involved. The first made a hole in the ceiling above the staircase, and the second whizzed over *my* head, not his.

Andy's back with his mother in Syracuse, where they're both undergoing family counseling which, as you might guess, I don't put a lot of hope in. But I do have a feeling that Andy might have begun his own change that night, sitting by his grandfather's side and absorbing something beyond words—something beyond wallowing in the mud of the past and worrying about who caused what and who owes what. Pop really took to Andy in that short time, and has high hopes for him. I think Andy took to Pop too.

Pop is in the process of buying Mr. Lindstrom's land, including Blood Red Pond, and although I gather Rachel still looks at him as a force from the dark side for having agreed to be her father's counsel in the now defunct lawsuit, I'd bet anything he offered considerably more than the property was worth, just so she and Andy could have an easier go of it.

So far I haven't told anybody about what I experienced in that hospital room, not even Bo, although I know I will, some night when we're sitting up talking into the wee hours of the morning. It's not that it's any big secret; it's just that, for now, I don't want to disturb the memory. I want to leave it tucked safely away.

I still have a good feeling about Mr. Lindstrom. From the little bits and pieces I know of his life, I'm pretty sure it hadn't been an easy one, and I get a nice glow inside when I think of him rising up from his tired and worn out body, looking down on his grandson and his friends, and returning Ethan's little wave—at least I like to think he did—before starting his return flight for home.

The other day I wandered into Ethan's room in search of another missing shirt, and on the way out I happened to glance up at Bo's Icarus painting. Right away it hit me that something was different about it. At first I couldn't tell what it was. Icarus looked pretty much the same as he ever did floating up there, and everything else looked just the way it always had. Then it dawned on me. The plowman, who I'd always seen as sinking into the dirt, wasn't doing that at all. What he was doing was pulling himself up *out* of the dirt. I don't know why I'd never seen it that way before. He looked as dense and weighted-down as ever, but I saw now how his legs and back were straining, pulling for all they were worth against the gravity. What's more, I could see how his neck muscles were tightening, and I knew it was only a matter of time before he'd pull his head up enough to get his first glimpse of the sky, and of Icarus gliding effortlessly above him. And I knew too, that once he got that glimpse, he'd never be the same.

So I'm thinking that in the end maybe we all get to be flyers. Maybe we're like that plowman, plodding along between the earth and the sky, and if we can only lift our heads enough we'll catch a glimpse of where it is we're headed. I've been thinking that a lot lately. I think it when I see Ethan lost in one of his Superman comic books or hear Mr. and Mrs. Michaelson thumping around in their basement. I think it too when I see the way Pop looks at Ethan and me each time we come through the door—or if I pick up the paper and happen to read about somebody dying.

And I think Bo had the right idea. That first time when Icarus fell out of the sky, it wasn't the end of his flight, but just the start of another one.

I like the thought.